WICKED BOSS

WILLOW FOX

Wicked Boss

Bratva Brothers Book 2

Copyright © 2022 by Willow Fox

Edited by Marla VanHoy

Cover Art by MiblArt

V2

ONE

Luka

The brunette situated across the bar stares down at her phone, scrolling through her newsfeed. Her bar stool turns as she swivels back and forth, unable to sit still.

The girl practically glows. She's radiant and sexy in a strapless dark red dress.

I want to rip it right off her.

Is she here for a date, or is she meeting friends? A girl like *her* doesn't show up alone. Not if she's smart and wants to play it safe.

I'm not here to pick up women, although the brunette has caught my gaze. I can't turn away from her.

I'm here with Mikhail having drinks, chilling while the night is young. The bar grows rowdy as the crowd fills in.

I watch her from a distance. I can't tear my gaze away, but she hasn't so much as looked up or glanced in my direction.

She's fixated on her damn phone.

What is it with kids these days? Okay, she's not technically a kid. She was carded upon entering the establishment, making her at least twenty-one, but she's young. She could be twenty-five, and I'm just bad with ages. But there's no way she's anywhere near my age—she isn't close to thirty, and I'm a few years shy of forty.

When did I get so fucking old?

The thought of settling down is non-existent. I'm not the kind of man to have a family. It would only endanger their lives. I don't make romantic connections.

I enjoy my youth, or at least what's left of it, falling into strange women's beds to show them what it's like to be ravished.

"Drinks?" Mikhail asks.

"On it," I say. I know what he likes, and I head to the bar. There's barely any room to stand, and the bartender disappears around back. Is he taking a cigarette break?

I exhale a heavy sigh. At this rate, I'll be here all night waiting to order a whiskey.

I don't wait around to ask permission. I step behind the counter like I own the place and grab two glasses and the finest whiskey on the top shelf.

"I'd like a Fuzzy Navel," the brunette says. She's a bit terse in her tone, and she finally glances up from her phone. The girl has the bluest eyes I've ever seen.

I finish pouring Mikhail's drink and glance her over. "You've been on your phone all night," I say.

She presses her lips tight. "You've been watching me?" She shifts, albeit uncomfortable under my scrutiny, like I'm judging her.

I grab an empty glass and the ingredients to fill her drink request.

There's no point in lying. I've already confessed to noticing that she's been preoccupied and alone. "It's difficult not to notice the most beautiful woman in the bar," I say, sliding her drink across the table. "It's on me," I say.

I carry the drinks I poured for Mikhail and myself back to the table.

"Took you long enough," Mikhail mutters.

"Sorry, I got distracted by that sexy brunette drinking alone."

Mikhail doesn't even try to be discreet as he peers past me at the girl in the scarlet gown. "She is quite the catch. Young. But you've always chased after tail half your age."

"And you don't?"

Mikhail's no saint. "We're not talking about me," he says and takes a swig of his whiskey. "You want to go home with her." It's not a question. He already knows the answer. It's not about what I want, though. I'm here keeping tabs on him, ensuring he has a decent time and gets home safely.

I'm not worried about him driving home sober. He's bratva and the Pakhan, the leader of the pack. My boss and mentor. What I'm concerned with is the Italian Mafia and the Colombian Cartel. Our two biggest enemies could be closing in on us at any moment.

I have to be alert and keep Mikhail protected. I'm his bodyguard, and if I'm not with him, Nikita is keeping close tabs on him.

"Go talk to her. I'll be fine. The place is crowded but docile."

He means there aren't any of our enemies drinking here tonight. I'm grateful. "If you insist," I say and don't wait for Mikhail to change his mind. I toss him the keys. He'll need them to get home tonight.

I can call a cab or a rideshare service to get back to the compound. I have my cell phone in my suit coat pocket and my wallet in my pants. I'm overdressed for the bar, but I've removed my suit coat and slung it over my arm.

I'm not at the table with Mikhail for more than a few seconds, downing my whiskey before heading back to the bar.

The bartender is still nowhere in sight. Did he bail?

Blue eyes glances up from her phone as I head toward the bar. "I could use another one of these," she says. Like I'm supposed to remember what she ordered.

If I were a bartender, I'm not sure that I'd have kept every customer's drink in my head. But it was just one extra to remember. And she's unforgettable.

"A Fuzzy Navel," I say and slip behind the bar. I make her a second glass and slide it to her before I come around to the other side. "Where's your boyfriend?" I ask.

She brings the drink to her lips and glances me over. "You mean my friend who stood me up?" She gestures toward the couple a few feet away, making out against the wall.

"They should get a room," I say.

She downs her drink and then moves to stand. "I should just go. Call it a night."

"The night's still early. It's Friday, and what do you have planned when you get home?" I imagine she'll climb into bed and go to sleep alone.

"A hot bubble bath if I leave now," she says and glances at her watch. She avoids my heated stare, and her cheeks burn, the longer I make eye contact with her.

It's difficult to hear one another over the commotion from the crowd. I lean in, my lips brushing against her ear. "And that's what you'd rather be doing tonight?" I ask, making sure she can hear me.

I swear I feel her shudder.

Her breathing deepens, and her eyes darken as she stares into my gaze. "No," her voice squeaks.

She gulps and licks her dry lips. A soft puff of air spills out. "Don't you have to bartend?"

I glance toward the bar and give her an award-winning grin. "I think they've got it covered."

She shifts against the stool, and I swear she's rubbing her inner thighs together, rocking slightly, applying pressure to just the right spot.

I tangle my fingers in her hair, brushing the curls behind her neck. My touch is soft and soothing. "So, you'd rather be in a bubble bath right now than here, enjoying the music and the atmosphere?" I whisper.

"It's not so bad," she confesses.

A grin spreads across my face. "Good. Do you want to shoot pool? I can show you how if you've never played."

"Sure."

"I'm Luka," I say, introducing myself.

"Hannah."

I take her hand and guide her off the stool. It's been a while since I played, but I can impress her even rusty.

I reach for the rack and set up the table. "Have you ever played?" I ask.

"Once or twice."

I grab the balls and put them into the rack, setting the game up. "Do you want to break?" I ask.

"That's when I start?" she asks curiously.

I get the feeling I'm being played. "Yes." I consider making a wager, suggesting I take her out if she wins, but I don't date. That's not who I am.

"Okay," Hannah says.

I gather the cue sticks and hand one to her. I grab the chalk and show her how to apply it to the pool cue tip before handing the chalk to her to use.

"Don't hit the eight ball in until the end. And you have to call the pocket."

"That's a lot of rules to remember." She puts her empty glass on a nearby table.

"Do you want another drink?" I ask.

"Are you trying to liqueur me up so I lose?"

I chuckle under my breath. "Never said I was a gentleman."

She bites down on her bottom lip and aims her shot, glancing back at me over her shoulder. "If I win, you buy the next round of drinks."

I can live with that wager. "You're on."

The girl is badass and a pool shark. I don't get a single shot. She knocks one ball in after another, gaining a second, a third, and fourth turn, before calling the pocket for the eight ball.

I don't like to lose, especially to a girl. "Hard to believe you've only played once or twice."

"Once or twice—a week," Hannah says, having left out that important tidbit earlier.

"What are you drinking?" I ask. I don't plan on going easy on her on the next round. She's good, but I don't lose.

"Same as earlier," she says.

I don't like leaving her alone, not even for a minute. Another man could swoop in and capture her attention. I'm quick and hurry to the bar, ordering her another Fuzzy Navel. She's across the room, and it's difficult to see her with the crowd tonight.

I'm back as quickly as I can be, and already, some dumbass is trying to vie for her affection. No chance in hell, buddy.

"You're hot," the short, blond stranger says, ogling Hannah.

My breath caresses her ear as I lean in to ensure that she can hear me, along with the idiot trying to gain her attention. "Hey, babe. Here's your drink," I say, handing it to her.

I rest my hand on her lower back possessively. She's not mine, but I intend to change that tonight.

"Thanks," she breathes a sigh of relief and sips her drink.

When the guy standing not more than a foot away doesn't seem to get the hint, she grabs me by the tie and pulls my head down toward her lips.

Her boldness surprises me, but it's refreshing even if she is doing it just to get rid of that pitiful man attempting to flirt with her.

She's the hottest girl in the room. I'm lucky that she hasn't told me to walk away. She is way out of my league.

Her lips cover mine, and I pull her tighter, harder, closer. I want to devour her.

My fingers pull her tight against me. She tastes like strawberries, and I'm starving.

The music blares overhead, the beat quick and fast, making it hard to concentrate with my heart pounding from her mouth latched onto mine. I want to fuck her but not here. She's too good for the bathroom or a quick lay in an alley.

The girl wears sophistication like it's a crown, and she's queen.

Our kisses are fevered and full of passion. With every breath exchanged between us, my head fills high above the clouds like floating on air. It's almost as if she is a drug and I'm an addict.

Hannah finally pulls back and runs a hand through her unkempt hair, breathing heavily. "Thank you."

"For the drink or for helping you ditch that fool?"

Her cheeks burn, and she smiles weakly, glancing down. Is she embarrassed about the kiss? What sane, hot-blooded male wouldn't want to kiss her?

"You're welcome," I say, not needing further explanation. "How about another round of pool?" I ask.

"Let me guess, you want to go first?"

"Seems only fair since I didn't get a turn."

Bringing the glass to her lips, she takes a swig. "Sure, you can go ahead and try to beat me."

Challenge accepted.

Hannah lifts her phone and unlocks the camera app. "Come here," she says and takes another gulp of her drink before putting it on the edge of the pool table.

I shake my head and wiggle my finger at her. "No chance." I have my reasons why I hate being in front of a camera, not that she needs to know any of them.

"What do you mean, no? Are you three?" Hannah laughs and grabs my arm. "Smile."

She lifts the phone and wraps an arm around my shoulders, pulling me closer for a photo.

I force a smile. It's not that I'm not enjoying my time with her, but I don't know who will see the photo, and I've done what I can to keep a low profile.

Hannah glances at the picture, unconvinced that she's done. "Another one," she says, and this time I give her a genuine smile if only to get her to stop with the pictures. I would never have thought she was the type who liked photographing every moment of her life.

She snaps two photographs, and then I plant my lips on hers, and she snaps one more. The world momentarily disappears around us as I pull her against me. Her body is warm and melts into my embrace.

"Do you want to get out of here?" I ask, breaking apart the kiss long enough to speak.

Hannah nods, and I take her hand, leading her out the front entrance. She pulls out her keys, her hands shaking. "I've never done this before."

The look on my face must give away my surprise. Is she a virgin?

"I mean gone home with a stranger."

I walk with her outside into the cold. Spring is just on the cusp, but it doesn't feel warm yet. "We're not quite strangers. You know my name." She's right, though, we don't know anything else about each other. Well, I know she's good at pool, and if we ever play on teams, I want her on mine.

Hannah is flustered, and I'm the reason for her nervousness.

"We don't have to do this," I say, resting my hands on hers. "We can just call it a night. Enjoy the moment that we had together."

She whimpers under her breath. "I want this. I'm just stupid nervous."

"Stupid nervous?" I ask, the grin widening across my face. "That's a new one." I haven't heard anyone use that terminology before. Then again, the members of the bratva would never admit they're nervous, and they're just about the only people I ever hang around with.

Hannah is a nice change of pace, even if it's only for one night.

There's an innocence to her. A sweet perfection that once shattered can never be made whole.

When we're done, she'll never be the same.

I'll ruin her in the best possible way.

TWO

Hannah

Three Years Later...

"All this wedding planning is tiresome. You're lucky that you're not married," I say. I change out of my scrubs. It's Friday, and I should be relishing that the weekend is here, but I have to work tomorrow.

The workday is over, but I'm not ready to go home and face Mark or my toddler, Bay.

Madisyn shoots me a look. "Planning your wedding is supposed to be fun."

"Well, it's not. Mark doesn't want any involvement. He's leaving everything up to me, which is good because we're not fighting, but I also find it stressful. Sometimes it would be nice for someone else to have an opinion about something wedding-related, other than me."

"I can help, not that I've ever planned a wedding, but I'm sure I can vet your vendors for the big day," Madisyn says.

I chuckle under my breath. "What are you going to do, run a background check on them? That sounds a bit drastic, Madisyn, even for you."

"I meant look at their past clients and reviews for their services. Or I could just come with you," Madisyn says. "I promise I'll only offer advice if you need it."

"Are you that desperate to get away from your boyfriend you just moved in with—what's his name, again?" I ask.

"Mikhail," she says, and her cheeks redden. "And no, I'm offering to help because I genuinely want to be there for you. You've been a good friend to me, and I want to return the favor."

"That's sweet. But if you want to be here for me, how about you tell me where you disappeared for the past two months?" I've been curious why she, out of the blue, was gone from work. She doesn't appear unhealthy or grieving, but maybe she had a private client whom she tended to on the concierge's request? No one at work knew where she'd vanished for the last several weeks.

But she kept her job and wasn't reprimanded as far as I know. I can't help but wonder what she'd gotten herself involved with.

"You wouldn't believe me if I told you," Madisyn says.

"Try me." I fold my arms across my chest. If we're friends, don't I deserve the truth?

"I used to work for the FBI. This job was just a cover."

She can't be serious.

Madisyn doesn't crack a grin, but that seems like the lamest excuse I've ever heard. It doesn't even make sense! "Fine, don't tell me the truth." I pull on my black winter boots, lacing them tight. There's no sense in staying mad at her for more than thirty seconds. Her business is entirely hers. If she doesn't want to tell me, I should respect her privacy.

"We should grab drinks after work. I'm dying to go dancing and have a night off. Mark is letting me have a girls' night. So, you have to come out," I say.

I've wanted a night out to unwind, and Madisyn is the perfect person to conquer the world alongside me. Plus, Bay has been waking up every night with nightmares, and I need a few hours of me-time or at least time to cut loose with my new bestie and chill.

Quickly, she changes out of her scrubs and asks me a dozen questions like am I letting him watch my daughter, Bay.

Of course, who else would be watching her? He's going to be her father. And while he's not super excited about diaper duty, he's a responsible adult.

Besides, we can't bring Bay to a bar or a nightclub.

I grab my phone from my locker. I can't help but boast about my little girl, how much she's grown, and how adorable she is. The kid is the one accomplishment I'm genuinely proud of, raising her and doing it on my own.

Madisyn pulls on her shoes and grabs my phone, cruising through my photos.

"You'd better not have any naked pictures on here," she warns.

Naked pictures? Mark wouldn't be caught dead taking off his shirt for a photo, let alone being naked. He's got a great body, but he has more issues than a magazine subscription.

"It's nothing you haven't seen, and no, Mark is a bit of a prude." I've tried to suggest we take some naughty photos and try some toys in the bedroom, but he's always against everything I come up with. He enjoys the same vanilla ice cream every time he gets to the ice cream shop.

I'm trying to be nice. That's like the understatement of the century.

"That's too bad," Madisyn says and gasps. She drops my phone against the bench, and it hits with a thud on the ground.

I just bought that phone a month ago. I slug her on the arm. Could she be any more careless? "Madisyn! If you break my phone, you're paying to replace it."

Madisyn grimaces and bends down to grab the phone. Flipping it over, she examines it. "Who is this guy?"

My breath catches in my throat when she brings up the selfie of my one-night stand. Luka and I grabbed a photo together before we went back to my place.

Exhaling a nervous breath, I snatch the phone back. "Bay's father. My hot one-night stand. I should delete that picture, but I thought Bay might want to see it one day."

"And he's not in Bay's life. Why?" Madisyn asks. She doesn't avoid the tough questions.

I run a hand through my hair. My stomach is filled with butterflies. Just talking about him, makes me nervous. There's also anger that bubbles up under the surface because he lied to me, and I fell for it.

"The dick lied to me, said he worked at the bar. It's not like I even know if Luka is his real name. It's for the best," I say, wanting to drop the subject. I'm getting married in a few short months, and Luka will always just be a distant memory of the past.

Madisyn clears her throat. "I know him, Hannah. He works with Mikhail. His name is Luka Ivanov."

The breath is stolen from my lungs, and I slump onto the bench, needing a minute to sit. "How long?" I rasp. Sweat beads at my forehead, and I hang my head forward, trying to exhale through my mouth while my stomach churns.

She slumps down beside me, a hand on my back. "A few months. I had no idea; what do you want me to do?" Madisyn asks.

"I'm going to be sick." Tonight is supposed to be fun, a girls' night away from the house.

"Just breathe," she says, settling me down with deep breaths. "Focus on breathing in through your nose and out through your mouth."

"It's not working." I'm trembling. My entire body is filled with a plethora of energy that I can't seem to release.

Adrenaline.

"Look at me, Hannah." Her voice is strong and steady, and while my vision wavers, she's my rock.

I glance up at her, and my breathing calms just a bit.

"Good," she says. "Now exhale."

I release a heavy sigh and run my hands through my hair. Already, I'm less spacy and more grounded.

"Do you get panic attacks often?" Madisyn asks.

"That wasn't—"

Her disapproving glare forces me to shut my mouth.

"No," I say. I wouldn't have classified it as a panic attack, but it was something that I didn't want to experience again. "Sorry about that."

"You don't need to apologize," Madisyn says. She grabs her purse and her phone. "How about we meet downstairs in ten? I want to call home and let Mikhail know that I will be late."

"Okay. Can you not mention to him about Luka?"

A wide grin splays across her face. "That's what I was going to open with. Do you mean I shouldn't?"

Gosh, she's cheeky. I purse my lips together. "I know you're joking."

"Relax. I won't say anything to Mikhail about Luka being your baby daddy."

I grimace at her use of the terminology. "Can we not do that? Please." I stand and grab my purse, shoving my phone back inside. "But eventually, I need to talk to Luka. But let's not call him my baby daddy. Okay?"

"Do you want me to invite him out tonight?" Madisyn asks.

"To girls' night?" My voice catches in my throat. That's the worst idea. I'm not ready to see him after three years. I don't have decent clothes on or my hair and makeup done. Not that it should matter. I'm engaged, but I still want to look presentable. Okay, not that I'd tell Madisyn, but I want to look knockout gorgeous when I meet with Luka.

Madisyn heads for the door. "On second thought, I'd rather be a fly on the wall, not a spectator at the table. Things could get dicey."

My jaw drops, and I choke on her words. There is no chance that Madisyn will be joining us when I drop the news on Luka that our one little tryst ended up with an eight-pound baby girl nine months later.

"Yeah, you're not invited when I tell Luka he's Bay's father."

"Fair enough," Madisyn says, holding her hands up as a mock surrender. She doesn't sound the least bit offended, and I'm not intending to insult her, but it's not a conversation to be discussed with friends when you drop that kind of anvil on a one-night stand.

"Ten minutes?"

"Yeah," I say, and she heads out, phone in hand. I assume she's going to talk to her boyfriend.

I run a comb through my hair and add a bit of lipstick before heading downstairs. Madisyn ought to be ready by now. I glance at my phone. There are no missed calls. No texts from Mark. He's not the kind of boyfriend to check-in or text me during the day. I chalk it up to the fact that he knows I'm busy and don't have time for chit-chat.

I dial his cell phone, and it takes three rings before Mark picks up the call.

"Everything okay?" he asks.

"Yeah, I just wanted to say hi."

"I'm kind of busy right now," Mark says. "Bay's still at preschool. I'll swing by and get her on my way home. I didn't forget."

"Okay, thank you." I always feel like a hindrance when I call.

He ends the call without so much as a goodbye. "Yeah, I love you too," I mutter to myself. I try to be understanding. I recognize that he's swamped, that this is the busy time of year for his job.

It still sucks that I feel like a second thought if even that. Maybe a third.

I'm probably just hormonal and need a night away from Mark to have fun, chill out, and unwind.

THREE

Luka

"Any chance I can convince you to go out tonight?" I ask, poking my head into Mikhail's office.

"Madisyn isn't going to let me go prowl the town with you," Mikhail says. "But she just called and is having a girls' night out with one of her work friends. I want you to be their chaperone."

"Chaperone?"

That isn't what I had in mind for tonight, babysitting his girlfriend and making sure that she stays out of trouble.

"You don't trust Madisyn?" I step farther into the office and close the door behind myself. While she's not home to overhear our conversation, I don't want any other men to start talking. That's how rumors spread.

Mikhail's dark gaze hardens. "She's pregnant, and with the cartel out there, and the mafia, I'd feel better if she has a bodyguard. Besides, there are enough creeps out there to worry about who aren't trying to get to me. I need to know that she's safe."

"Sir, I don't think she will appreciate us showing up to her girls' night out."

Does he not understand the point of a girls' night?

Madisyn wants to be left alone, and he doesn't need to worry about her loyalties. The girl is enthralled with him. There's no chance that she's going to stray.

"I didn't say we. I said you."

I grumble under my breath. "Great." If I'm lucky, she won't throw a drink in my face, but Madisyn can be a bit hot-headed and isn't going to take it lightly that I have orders to watch her at the bar.

"I'll make sure she only orders virgin drinks, sir." I glance at my watch. "Do you know what bar she's going to?" It would make it easier to know where I have to go to keep an eye on her.

Mikhail glances at his phone and texts me the address. "Take Nikita with you if you want to look inconspicuous."

"Madisyn isn't stupid, sir. She'll know we're there to watch her. It's better if I go alone."

"Whatever you want, just make sure she gets home safely."

———

I sit in a booth near the back of the bar, my back pressed up against the wall, my gaze drawn toward the door. I'm watching and waiting for Madisyn to show up.

I intend to stay out of the way, let the girl have some fun, and if trouble shows up, then I'll be on hand to help.

Madisyn heads inside the bar, pushes her oversized sunglasses atop her head and makes her way to the bar.

"Hannah," I whisper, recognizing the girl following in behind Madisyn. She's worked my stomach up into a knot. The girl doesn't look a day older than when I last saw her. Sure, she's not wearing that dynamite red dress, but she still looks hot in tight jeans and a baby blue sweater.

Madisyn leans forward to grab the bartender's attention and puts in an order. I stalk across the bar, unable to tear my gaze away from Hannah.

The last time I saw her, we were tearing her living room apart in a blaze of passion.

We stumble through her front door, and I kick it shut with my foot. I spin her around, our lips fused as I pin her against the wooden surface.

She shivers and moans as I kiss a path down her neck.

Her fingers are tangled in my hair, pulling me closer before she takes control, pushing me backward, her lips nibbling mine.

A wry grin spreads across my face. Her hands rip at the buttons on my shirt, pulling the material free.

I didn't think she had it in her, my little firecracker.

She stares at my chest, her hands raking over my skin, slow and attentive.

I lift her off the ground with ease, backing her up against the wall. Clumsily, we fumble from one wall to the next. A picture frame falls to the ground. The frame splinters as we wrestle aimlessly, unable to tear apart for even an instant.

She heeds my roughness and isn't afraid of my strength.

Her breathing is deep and raspy, and my cock twitches wanting to feel her lips wrapped around the shaft.

I shake away the distant memory. Getting hot and bothered isn't going to help tonight. She's off-limits if she's Madisyn's friend. Besides, I have a rule that I don't fuck the same girl twice.

The last thing I want is to end up tied down.

But why am I striding across the bar to ensure that she notices me?

I want to be seen. I want her to remember me because I was the best she's ever had. I should stay on my ass, hidden in the back, and keep Madisyn from blowing up at me.

Except I can't do that.

While most of the girls I don't remember their names after a few months, Hannah is different. I still remember her apartment and the scent of cinnamon and spice that greeted me at the door. The taste of strawberries on her lips and the feel of her tightness wrapped around my cock, pulsating as she moaned.

We made a mess of that place, destroyed her furniture, broke her bed, and collapsed the wooden end table. It still brings a smile to my face, the passion that became blazing. We even had the cops called twice for a noise complaint.

Her cheeks flame.

Oh yeah, she remembers me.

FOUR

Hannah

What is Luka doing here?

"Did you tell your boyfriend?" I can't help but accuse Madisyn. Why else would Luka show up at the bar and stalk his way toward us?

I shouldn't have trusted her with my secret!

"Only that I was going out for drinks with a friend." She spins around on her heels and pokes Luka in the chest as he approaches.

"What the hell are you doing? Did Mikhail send you?" Madisyn's fuming. "Does he not trust me? Is that why you're spying on us?"

Luka clears his throat and forces a smile at me before returning his attention to Madisyn. "Take it down a notch."

"I would if you weren't being a barbarian," Madisyn says.

"What have I done to offend you?" Luka asks. He's calm, incredibly so for dealing with Madisyn, who is about to pound the shit out of him. But he's taller than she is and far more muscular. It wouldn't be difficult for him to subdue her if he wanted to.

"Other than showing up uninvited!"

He could be a bodyguard for celebrities or billionaires with his physique and roughness. I don't know what he does for a living. It's not something that we discussed the last time I saw him. We were too involved in ripping off each other's clothes.

"You're making a scene," Luka warns. His tone is threatening, disapproving of her behavior. But he hasn't laid a finger on her. He raises his arm, gesturing the bartender over. He'd started to approach earlier, but one look at the heated exchange between them, and he vanished as though it were a lover's quarrel.

Thankfully, it wasn't. As far as I know, Luka and Madisyn aren't an item. She's happily dating Mikhail.

But I don't quite know Luka's status. I never asked Madisyn if he was seeing someone. It shouldn't matter. I'm engaged. I'm supposed to be happily planning my wedding. I've been planning the wedding, but the happy part is debatable at times.

I'm sure it's just my nerves, cold feet, and Luka Ivanov, my daughter's father, is staring back at me.

"What do you want?" Luka asks.

"Excuse me?" I'm taken aback by his question.

Luka gestures at the bartender waiting to take our orders. "What do you drink? It's on me," he says, offering to foot the bill, at least for this round.

"Damn right it's on you," Madisyn says.

His gaze flinches, and he shoves his hand into his back pocket, retrieving his wallet. He opens the black bifold and grabs his credit card, sliding it across the bar top to pay for our drinks.

"I'll have a Fuzzy Navel," I say, giving the bartender my order.

"Anything for you?" the bartender asks Madisyn.

"Ginger ale," Madisyn says and slips out of Luka's grasp.

"Where are you going?" Luka asks.

Madisyn groans and throws her hands up into the air. "The bathroom!" She storms off toward the back of the bar, and he pushes himself away from the bar.

"Give the girl space and some privacy," I say.

He exhales a heavy sigh and leans back against the bar.

I sit on the stool, our knees brushing against one another. "How have you been?" I ask, trying to play it cool. I mean, what the hell am I supposed to do? I don't know anything about him, and I'm not sure how to drop the: *you're a father* bomb on the guy.

The moment the bartender returns with my drink, I sip it hastily, using it as a temporary distraction.

"I've been good," Luka says. He's not a man who smiles much, but the corners of his lips quirk upwards. "What about you? I didn't know you and Madisyn were friends."

"Coworkers," I say. However, I'd like to think that we're becoming friends. "What are you doing here? Is it because her boyfriend is jealous and can't stand the thought of her having fun without him?"

"He sent me to keep an eye on her and make sure that she doesn't do anything stupid."

"She's not going to do anything stupid. You're the one being stupid."

He chuckles at my remark.

It's not supposed to be funny, but I'm standing up for my friend, even if I sound childish in my rebuke.

"Relax. I didn't come here to get into a boxing match. I'm here as your designated driver."

I roll my lips together. "The subway's only a few blocks from here. There's also a cab. And I don't need a designated driver, and by the looks of it, Madisyn isn't ordering alcohol. You can go home."

Does he think that we can't take care of ourselves? I've been looking after myself for as long as I can remember and taking care of my child without anyone else's help.

He holds up his hands. "I'm not looking to start a fight," Luka says.

"It's a little late for that," I mutter.

He glances away, avoiding eye contact. His attention is on the back hallway, where Madisyn disappeared a few minutes earlier to use the restroom.

Is he enthralled with Madisyn?

"Do you have a thing for her? Because she's dating someone," I say. I down the rest of my drink and gesture the bartender over for another. If I'm going to be dealing with Luka, I'll need quite a few more of these. All the better if it's on his tab.

"She's dating my boss, and no, I don't have a *thing* for anyone."

My mouth is dry, and I lick my lips, glancing away. "Okay," I say and expel a soft puff of air. "You're cranky. Someone missed their afternoon nap."

"I don't nap."

Well, maybe he should. It works for Bay when she's crabby.

Madisyn struts out of the bathroom, her head held high as she breezes past Luka and grabs the bar stool, plopping down beside me. "Did you miss me?" Her attention is entirely on me, and she hasn't feigned a glance in Luka's direction, even though he's hovering and right next to me.

She's ignoring him.

Will that work?

"Like you wouldn't believe," I say. Next time she runs to the bathroom, we're going together.

Luka takes the hint and scoots out of our way. "I'll be over there if you girls need anything," he says and gestures toward the corner of the bar.

"We won't," I say and breathe a sigh of relief when he heads to his seat in the back of the bar at a table by himself. It's a bit pathetic that he's stuck here, watching Madisyn.

I wait until he's out of earshot. "What the hell, Madisyn? Why is he following you?"

She grabs her ginger ale and takes a sip, avoiding my heated stare.

"Well?"

"Mikhail is a bit overprotective. He's worried because I'm pregnant. At least I think that's why he sent his bodyguard to keep an eye on us."

"You're pregnant?" I squeal.

Her eyes widen, and she gestures for me to keep it down. "Yes, but I'm not telling anyone. At least not at work. You have to keep it a secret."

Who am I going to tell? "Of course. I promise," I say, giving her my pinky.

She laughs, glancing at my hand gesture before locking pinkies with me. "I feel like I'm in the third grade all over again. Did you talk to Luka about Bay?"

"You do remember her name." I laugh and glance in Luka's direction. He's seated in the back, behind Madisyn. It's not difficult to glance past her subtly without him noticing. "No, it didn't feel like the right time."

"It's never going to be the right time. And I swear I didn't invite him tonight."

"I know. It was obvious with the fight between the two of you that you didn't expect him to be here. Are you mad at Mikhail for sending him?"

"I'm not happy about it," Madisyn says. She finishes her ginger ale and gestures the bartender over. "I'll have a Shirley Temple."

She grins and waves at Luka.

What is she up to?

The bartender spends a few minutes preparing our drinks before sliding them across the bar top. "Thanks," I say, grabbing mine, enjoying the slight buzz. I probably shouldn't have skipped lunch.

FIVE

Luka

For five minutes, can Madisyn stay out of trouble?

Exhaling a heavy sigh, I stand and approach the two girls. I should stay far away from Hannah, but I can't. The truth is I don't want to. Mikhail has finally settled down, and he's happy.

I never thought I'd want that life, but seeing the two of them together, it's hard not to be jealous.

The lights are dim in the bar, and the crowd grows loud. I stalk up to the troublesome duo and reach for Madisyn's drink.

"What are you doing?" Hannah asks, sliding off the barstool. She steps between her friend and me, blocking Madisyn.

Hannah likely doesn't know that Madisyn is pregnant. And it's not my place to tell her.

I reach around Hannah and snatch the red drink, sniffing the liquid. It's hard to tell if there's alcohol in it or not. I take a sip.

It's sweet and not the least bit strong or bitter. I don't taste any hint of alcohol.

"It's a Shirley Temple, asshole," Madisyn says and smacks me in the arm. "Give me back my drink."

I relinquish the glass and step back, out of the way.

Hannah folds her arms across her chest. "Are you going to explain yourself?"

Great, she's defending Madisyn. I gesture the bartender over and order a whiskey. Madisyn's glass is still full, and Hannah is sipping her girly drink.

That night is etched into my mind, and I can't help but fantasize about undressing Hannah and fucking her.

Did she make that big of an impression on me? I shift uncomfortably at the thought, and my gaze wanders down over her cleavage.

"She's not supposed to have alcohol," I say and meet her stare. "I wanted to make sure the bartender didn't mess up her order."

Hannah rolls her eyes. "It's not up to you what she orders."

While she's right, it is up to me to protect Madisyn. And if Hannah is with her tonight, then she's my responsibility too.

Madisyn sips her Shirley Temple and grabs Hannah's hand, dragging her onto the dance floor. I hold Hannah's seat at the bar, watching their unattended drinks and ensuring no one messes with them.

The girls dance and shoo off several men who show interest in them. I keep an eye out to make sure that they're not being bothered or harassed by anyone as I sip my whiskey and order a second.

Every so often, I glance at my watch and am relieved when Madisyn comes up to tell me she's done and ready to head home. That's my cue to drive her back to the compound. "Does Hannah have a ride home?" I ask.

"I'm right here," Hannah says and jabs me in the side, perturbed that I was asking Madisyn instead of directing my question at Hannah.

"Well, do you have someone picking you up?" I ask. I'm not keen on her driving home. She's had a few drinks, and I've seen her attempt to walk from the dance floor to the bar. The girl isn't the least bit steady on her feet. Although it could be the heels that she's wearing.

"No, I'm planning on driving home." Hannah pulls on her coat and grabs her car keys from her pocket.

"Nonsense. I'll drop you off on our way." I reach for her keys in her palm, and she closes her hand.

Madisyn is buttoning her coat, watching the exchange between us but not interfering. There's a hint of a smile on her lips, and I'm not sure what she finds funny.

"You're not driving home," I say. "Let me drive you or get you a cab."

Hannah emits a heavy sigh and zips up her coat. "Fine. If you want to drive me home, have at it. I live across town."

"The same place you lived in a few years ago?" I ask.

Her cheeks flame, and her eyes widen. "Luka!" she snarls and smacks my arm.

"What did I say?" I ask. Why are women so difficult to read? What did I do?

Madisyn's grin has only further grown on her face. She grabs her purse. "Are you two love birds ready?"

Hannah scowls at me, and I close the tab and pay the bartender for our drinks before leading both ladies outside to my vehicle. Madisyn climbs into the backseat, letting Hannah sit up front with me.

I'm not sure whether I should thank her or not.

While I don't remember the address of her apartment, I do know the general whereabouts. I shouldn't recall quite so easily where she lives. I've slept with dozens of women, and most I wouldn't remember if I walked past them on the street, let alone where they reside.

But Hannah was different.

I'm not sure why. Maybe it was because she kicked my ass at pool. I didn't let her win. I never even had a chance.

From the first moment that I spoke with her, it was evident that she is way out of my league. We're from different worlds. She probably wants kids, a family, and a white picket fence.

"I'll need your address when we get close," I say and head in the vicinity of her apartment complex.

"You don't remember?" Hannah jokes and pulls the seatbelt low and tight across her lap, securing the buckle.

I pull out of the parking lot of the bar. Madisyn is impeccably quiet. I glance in the rearview mirror, and she's staring out the side window. I'll take it as a win. Hannah probably tired her out on the dance floor.

She points to the red brick building as we near the apartment complex. "I'm in there," she says. I pull the SUV over to the side of the road and put the vehicle in park.

I glance back at Madisyn. She's playing on her cell phone in the backseat. "I will walk Hannah inside and make sure she gets home okay. Do you want to sit up front?"

"Sure," Madisyn says. She climbs into the front seat, and I leave the vehicle running, letting her stay warm. She locks the doors, and I hurry to the front entrance with Hannah, my hand on her lower back as I escort her to the door and inside the building.

"You didn't have to walk me all the way home," she says with a nervous laugh.

"It's the least I could do after tonight." I don't deny that it was a disaster. Seeing her again has been the highlight of my evening.

Once we're inside the lobby, Hannah hits the button for the elevator. She shuffles her feet and exhales a heavy sigh.

"You don't have to walk me to my apartment door. Madisyn is waiting for you," Hannah says. Her voice is soft and tentative. She licks her lips, the ones that taste remarkably like strawberries. I want to kiss her, but we've been battling all night.

It doesn't feel right.

I'm not the kind of guy who takes advantage of a woman. And she's been drinking.

"She's in a warm vehicle. The doors are locked. I want to make sure that you get home safely," I say.

The elevator doors open, and we step inside together. She hits the button for the third floor. "Listen, I'm sorry about tonight."

"About tonight?" She laughs, and there's an edge to her tone. She's not happy. She's pissed. But I'm not sure what I did yet. "What about lying to me several years ago? Are you sorry about that?"

"Lying to you," I whisper, trying to recall what I might have said that wasn't true and must have offended her.

She expels a heavy breath and blows the hair out of her face with her breath. The elevator dings, and the double doors open.

A reprieve.

Hannah bolts out of the elevator and is two steps ahead of me. I'm taller, so she's practically racing to her door to leave me in the dust.

"I'm sorry," I say. Although honestly, I don't quite know what I'm apologizing for.

She approaches 3B, her apartment door. It's bright red, just like the outside of the building. All the doors are painted a brick red. I don't remember the color, but I also had her pinned between me and the door. I remember most of that night involving her naked, writhing beneath me.

"Forget it," she mutters under her breath. "It's all in the past." She digs into her pocket for her keys and shoves them into the door but doesn't turn the lock.

"Listen, I truly am sorry if I said or did something back then to offend you. I'd like to make it up to you. The two of us could go out sometime, grab a drink."

The front door swings open, and a gentleman with sandy brown hair and glasses breathes a sigh of relief. "Oh good, you're home. Bay is running a fever, and I don't know what to do."

He doesn't even seem to notice me. It's probably for the best. I didn't show up at her front door to bring drama into her life.

Hannah exhales a breath. "Thanks for the ride," she says, glancing up at me.

"Oh, did you take a rideshare home? Do I need to pay him?" He reaches into his back pocket for his wallet.

"I'm just one of Madisyn's friends," I say and gesture to the elevator. "I should get back to the vehicle. She's waiting inside, and we're parked out front."

"Thanks for giving her a lift."

I didn't do it for him. I didn't even know there was a *him*.

Who is he?

Her boyfriend? Her husband?

And who the hell is Bay?

Does Hannah have a kid?

SIX

Hannah

That wasn't how I wanted Luka to discover that I have a daughter, or rather that we have a child together.

Although it's unlikely he realizes that Bay is his child. I shuffle inside to deal with Bay while Mark closes the door and locks it.

Luka is gone.

I should be relieved, but I'm not the least bit happy, other than that I saw him tonight. And it's a mixed bag of emotions—everything from excitement to anger courses through me when I think about Luka Ivanov.

Bay is already in my bed, buried under a quilt. She doesn't feel feverish, and I grab the thermometer to get a quick reading of her temperature.

No fever.

I lift Bay into my arms and put her into her bed for the night before closing her bedroom door.

"Bay's fever broke," I say. Whatever Mark did must have helped. "You could have called me. I'd have come home early if I knew she was sick."

"I didn't want to bother you," Mark says and plops down on the sofa. "I gave her a popsicle and some children's Tylenol. It seems to have done the trick."

"Thank you," I say and grab a seat next to him on the sofa.

He reaches for the remote, turning on the television. I seem to be the furthest thought from his mind.

"Can we talk?" I ask, pulling my legs up on the sofa. I grab the blue and purple throw blanket and drape it over my lap.

"About what?" Mark has barely glanced in my direction, his attention on the screen.

"Luka," I say.

"Who?" Mark glances at me.

"The guy who brought me home." It's like a band-aid that I have to rip off. Mark needs to know that Luka may end up in our lives, in Bay's life.

His brow furrows and his shoulders tense. "What about him?"

Is it jealousy that's gotten into him? I've never known Mark to be jealous.

"He's Bay's father," I say.

Mark turns his attention from the television and pauses the live feed with the DVR remote. "That's not funny."

"I'm not joking."

Mark deserves the truth. So does Luka. I just need to find the strength to tell Luka that he's Bay's father.

"What are you trying to say, Hannah? Because that guy, he's definitely not your type."

"Well, he was when I brought him home three years ago." I wince at my words. I didn't intend it to become a fight. That's the last thing that I want.

Mark is good to me. He's good for Bay, and he's stable. He'll be there for us through anything.

"Does he know he's Bay's biological donation?" Mark asks.

The way he says it makes me feel dirty and ashamed of what transpired between Luka and me. "I haven't told him yet. But I intend to."

"Don't." Mark stands and paces the length of the living room. The apartment isn't huge. It's a two-bedroom and the same home that I've had since I got a job at Steele Concierge Medical. It's not too far from work, and the building is kept up. I can also swing the rent, which isn't easy considering the cost of living in the city.

"I would have told him sooner if I could have tracked him down," I say. I plant my feet firmly on the ground, the blanket falling to the floor, and I don't bother to pick it up. "He deserves to know the truth, that he has a daughter."

"You don't even know the guy. You don't know anything about him!"

I grimace and fold my arms across my chest. "It's not your decision to make." I'm trying to do what's best for my daughter.

"The hell it isn't!" Mark stops and turns to face me. "You're marrying me. Bay will be my daughter. I'm the one raising her, not that—thug!"

I pinch the bridge of my nose and try and take a few calming breaths. I don't want to say anything that I might regret.

"We'll talk about this tomorrow. I'm going to bed." I stand and brush past Mark, heading for the bedroom.

Mark stomps his foot, and I swear he's about to have a temper tantrum. "I'm not done talking about it."

Why is he this way?

Difficult.

We've never fought about anything before today.

I run a hand through my hair and spin around to face him. "Fine. What if the situation were reversed and you had a kid out there? Are you telling me that you wouldn't want to know about it?"

There's no way he'd be happy with being kept in the dark.

"If it's what's best for my child, yes."

I take a step closer to Mark. "If this is about what's best for Bay, then having her father in her life seems like the answer."

He's fuming. "Don't go turning this around, Hannah. She has me. I'm the only father she needs. Not some deadbeat, scruffy bastard who probably can't keep a job."

He gets all that from one glance at Luka? "You're making a lot of assumptions."

"And you're making the biggest mistake regarding Bay."

My hands bunch into fists. The nerve of him, to think that he knows what's best. "Don't tell me how to raise my daughter."

"Our daughter," Mark corrects me.

I bite my tongue. She's not *his*, not yet.

"I don't get why you want him in our lives. He'll complicate things for you, Hannah. He could want custody."

"I'm done talking about this," I say and shrug out of his grasp, heading for the bedroom.

"Hannah!"

I head for the bedroom and abruptly shut the door before collapsing onto the mattress. For the first time, I miss this place being my own and having a room that I can disappear into and be left alone.

Mark doesn't follow. I'm relieved to have a few minutes of peace and quiet. I undress for bed and change into my pajamas before climbing beneath the covers and shutting off the bedroom light.

Tears spill onto my pillow. I wipe the remnants away, shifting against the mattress, trying to still my racing mind.

Sleep eludes me, and I'm left alone, grumpy, and out of sorts. Mark has never behaved like this before. He's never been jealous. What bug crawled up his ass?

I don't do well when I'm deprived of slumber.

———

The bedroom door squeaks open, and I roll onto my back as the morning light streams in through the blinds.

The smell of coffee wafts into the bedroom, further waking me.

My head hurts, and my stomach is doing somersaults.

Wonderful.

"Did you come to bed last night?" I ask.

Mark is in the bathroom, the door open, brushing his teeth.

I have to be at work shortly. Forcing myself out of bed, I stalk to the dresser and grab my clothes.

He spits his toothpaste in the sink, gargles with a dixie cup filled with water, and rinses the sink clean. "I fell asleep on the couch," he says, stepping out from the bathroom.

There's a heaviness in the room, a tension that seems to be stretching out like a rubber band. Eventually, it will snap.

I can't remember Mark ever falling asleep on the couch. "Are we fighting?" I don't want to be fighting with him. I'd like him to respect my decision and move on from what happened between us last night.

"Well, that depends. Are you still planning on telling that guy he's Bay's father?" Mark asks. He folds his arms across his chest, his shoulders tense and his nostrils flaring.

"You're mad."

"I'm not happy about it."

"Yeah, well, I'm not happy with you right now." I shuffle past him and slam the bathroom door shut on his heels.

"What did I do?" Mark's muffled reply echoes through the door.

Am I being unreasonable?

I'm not trying to be a bitch, but Luka has the right to know he has a daughter. I'd have reached out to him sooner if I could have, with his phone number. The digits he left had been smeared and gotten destroyed.

Mark is just trying to look out for me, for us as a family, but I can't ignore the past or the fact that the man has reappeared in our lives.

The timing sucks.

I quickly get dressed, brush my teeth, and hurry out of the bathroom past Mark. He doesn't seem to have moved an inch since I slammed the door on him.

"You're mad," Mark says.

"You're just now figuring that out? I can't do this right now. I have to go to work." I hastily head out of the bedroom. The television is on in the living room with cartoons playing on the screen. Bay is seated on the sofa, my favorite throw blanket curled up around her.

"Mama!" Bay says when she glances back at me.

"Good morning," I say and waltz over, hugging my little ray of sunshine. I squeeze her an extra second than usual, and she wiggles her way to freedom. "I have to go to work," I say and drop a kiss on her cheek.

"You're leaving her here, with me," Mark says.

His tone suggests that he's not happy about her staying behind and me going to work. I swear my headache is growing by the second.

"Do you want me to take her with me?" I ask. There's a daycare at the concierge center for staff members to utilize. She attends preschool during the weekday, but on weekends, I've taken her with me to the daycare, especially before I met Mark.

Maybe I'm putting too much responsibility on him with Bay.

I drop a kiss on her forehead. She's not the least bit warm—no runny nose. No fever. She's got a sippy cup next to her and seems to be doing fine this morning. If she is sick, daycare, even at the center, would require her to be sent home.

"No, I just want you to leave that barbarian alone." He gestures to the front door where he'd met Luka the previous night. "I don't want him in our life."

I can't deal with this right now. I'm running late as it is. "I have to go to work," I say, giving Bay another kiss before grabbing my keys and purse and bolting out the door.

———

"You look like hell," Madisyn says as I practically run into her as I rush toward the elevator.

"I feel like hell," I say.

"Too much to drink?" Madisyn takes a stab at the problem. She's far off base.

It's just the two of us in the elevator, and I'm grateful for the reprieve from Mark. Who would have thought going to work would be easier than dealing with a jealous fiancé?

I pull my hair back with an elastic band around my wrist. "No, Mark is pissed about Luka."

She cringes. "How come?" Madisyn asks.

"Luka walked me home," I say, leaving out all the dirty details that she's looking for, like the fact he met Mark and learned that I have a daughter.

The elevator dings, and the double doors open. Madisyn steps out and waits for me to accompany her. She's already in her scrubs and has her identification badge on her shirt. I still need to change into my work attire.

It turns out I'm later than I thought. I head down the hall, and Madisyn follows me as if she has nothing better to do. Doubtful. She probably just wants all the gossip.

"Luka was a hundred times grumpier after he dropped you off. Did you tell him about Bay?"

"What? No."

I hurry down the hallway and head in to get dressed. I'm mostly changed, but I don't typically wear my scrubs to work. Plus, I always keep an extra change of clothes handy if a patient gets sick on me. It wouldn't be the first time.

"Well, what happened?" Madisyn asks. She glances me over. "You look like hell, and so did he last night."

"Nothing. I mean, it should have been nothing. He walked me to my door. No big deal, right? Well, Mark opened it."

"Shit," Madisyn gasps, and her eyes widen. "Did Luka try to kiss you?"

I chuckle at her remark. "No, it was nothing like that. Mark mentioned that Bay had a fever, and Luka overheard. I guess he wasn't ready to find out that I have a kid."

"Or a fiancé!"

"Right." I chew on my bottom lip as I strip down and change clothes in haste. "Not sure how much longer that will last," I mutter.

"What?" Madisyn hears my remark.

Shit.

"Mark doesn't want me to tell Luka that Bay is his daughter." I slip on my sneakers before tying the laces. I shove my clean clothes into the locker and shut it, then drop my phone into my pocket.

"Why the hell not?" Madisyn folds her arms across his chest. "You have to tell him! He's the father, not Mark."

Does she think I don't realize that already? "Yeah, so we got into it last night. He slept on the couch."

"Yikes." Madisyn grimaces. "Anything I can do to help?"

I tug my bottom lip between my teeth and shake my head. There's nothing that I can think of that will fix this, except for giving into Mark, which I refuse to do.

Madisyn slaps me on the back. "Don't sweat it. He'll come around."

"Mark or Luka?" I ask with a nervous laugh. I'm not sure Mark will come around. That's one of his quirks. He's stubborn to a fault.

"Mark. I do not doubt that Luka will make a great father."

I exhale a heavy breath. "Yeah. How am I supposed to tell Luka when Mark will have a fit? I swear it's like having two toddlers at the house."

Madisyn gives me a genuine smile and grabs my hands. "How about you come by after work tonight? We can have dinner, and you can spend a little time with Luka."

"You're setting us up?" The girl is devious.

Madisyn squeezes my hands. "I'm trying to help. What you decide to tell him, that's entirely up to you. But it seems like you can't meet Luka somewhere without Mark getting upset. Am I right?"

"Mark will be upset if I tell Luka about Bay. It's not that I'm meeting him. He's jealous, but it's not the type of jealousy you'd think a man would have."

"What do you mean?" Madisyn asks.

I head to the hallway, needing to get started for the day and check on my patients. "Mark thinks Luka isn't my type. He's not possessive jealous. He seems more afraid of Luka interfering with our family's perfect little life."

"It's still a form of jealousy, and oh my gosh, Mark ought to be jealous of Luka. He's eye candy and a bad boy. I never knew you were into the troublesome ones."

A faint smile tugs at the corners of my lips. "Yeah, me either. He just noticed me at the bar a few years ago."

"I'll say." Madisyn grins. "I want all the details—later. I have to start my rounds."

"Tonight. But is it okay if I bring Bay?" I don't want to abandon her two nights in a row.

"Of course. I'll text you the address."

————

I'm relieved when I get off work and spend the evening with Madisyn. I should probably want to go home, spend time with Mark, and talk about our problems.

Mainly Luka.

But I'm not over Mark's drama and jealousy. A little time apart would be good for us. I text him that I'm having dinner over at Madisyn's.

He doesn't answer.

Typical.

I head into the apartment, and he's seated in front of the television watching sports while Bay is banging pots and pans around in the kitchen. At least the noise sounds like it's coming from the kitchen.

"Mama!" Bay squeals and runs toward me, dropping the metal pans to the floor, making a clanking sound.

I grimace from the noise but pull my favorite little toddler into my arms for a hug and several kisses. "I missed you," I say.

"Missed you," she says and clings to me as though her life depends on it. I lift her into my arms, and she keeps a tight hold around my neck.

I stalk across the room, trying to get Mark's attention. I don't want to fight with him. I ask, "Did you get my text?"

"Yeah. That's fine," Mark says. His attention is on the television. He's barely glanced in my direction.

"I'm going to take Bay with me. You're welcome to come," I say, inviting him. Although Madisyn didn't ask him to dinner, it feels wrong ditching him. If he agrees to come with me, I'll bring a dish and text her on the way.

"Who is going to be there?" Mark asks, glancing at me. He brings a glass of scotch to his lips and takes a swig.

He's never touched alcohol while we dated.

"Madisyn and her boyfriend, Mikhail."

"As long as that barbarian isn't going, I'm good here. I'll just watch the game. Have fun."

"Do you mean Luka?" I ask. "Because he has a name." I'm growing tired of his jealousy and his antics.

"Yeah, I don't want you taking Bay to see him."

"It's not your decision to make. She's my daughter, and he's her biological—"

"Donor," Mark interjects.

"I'm leaving," I say and head for the door. I put Bay down to bundle her up in her purple coat, hat, and gloves. I don't want to take a chance that she'll be cold outside.

Mark stands. "You didn't answer my question."

"I didn't realize that you asked one." I secure both gloves on Bay's hands before grabbing my coat off the hook.

He strides across the living room for the door. "Is Luka going to be there?"

"Honestly, I don't know." If Madisyn has her way, he'll be there, but he could have plans and not show up, which would be fine with me. I've had all the drama that I can deal with for one day.

"I don't want you taking Bay with you if Luka will be there." He shoves his palm against the front door, blocking us from leaving.

"Are you serious? I'm not doing this with you, Mark."
I button my coat and grab my keys. He's managed to
fully block the front door, his back to the entrance,
his arms folded across his chest. "Move."

He doesn't budge.

"Are you fucking kidding me?"

"Bay stays here with me. She likes watching
basketball." He glances past me, checking out the
scores on the screen.

"Really? Last I saw, she was playing in the kitchen by
herself." I lift Bay into my arms, protecting her.
There's no way in hell I'm leaving her here tonight
with Mark. What the hell has gotten into him?
"Move out of the way," I say.

"Why? So, you can play house with your new
boyfriend? He doesn't love you, Hannah. He won't
love you, not like I can. I'll always be there for you."

He grabs my arm, his fingers digging into my biceps.

"Don't do this," he says, his breath wreaking of
alcohol.

How much did he have to drink? I grimace. His grip
is forceful and strong. "Let go of me."

His hold doesn't lighten. "Do you think he wants you or anything to do with your little brat?"

"You don't know what you're saying, Mark. You're drunk." I elbow him in the stomach, forcing him to double over while I slip out of the apartment with Bay in my arms. I hurry down to the car, buckling her into the backseat.

I keep glancing over my shoulder, waiting to see if Mark follows us outside. He's not a man to let things go, and that worries me almost as much as his jealousy.

SEVEN

Luka

I swing by the concierge clinic and pick Madisyn up from work.

"Guess what!" Madisyn squeals as she climbs into the front seat. Her excitement is nauseating.

I barely got any sleep last night after learning that Hannah has a family. According to Madisyn, she's not married yet. But she might as well be, she's got a kid, and I'm not going to fuck up her perfect, happy family.

I don't know why the blue-eyed brunette got under my skin, but I can't stop thinking about her.

"What?" I grumble.

"I invited Hannah over for dinner."

"What do you mean you invited Hannah over for dinner? Did you ask Mikhail?"

"I don't have to ask his permission. He's not my keeper," Madisyn says. "Besides, he'll be fine with it."

For being a former FBI agent, Madisyn can have her head in the clouds at times.

"He's not keen on inviting strangers into the compound."

"They're not strangers," she says. "Hannah is my friend, and it's just her and her daughter."

"Bay?" I ask, remembering the little girl's name from the night before. Should she be bringing Bay out if she's sick? Didn't that idiot mention something about the kid having a fever?

I shouldn't hate the man Hannah is involved with. It's none of my business whom she dates or shares a bed with.

Madisyn nods slowly. Like she's working through something in her head, but I can't fathom what. The girl likes to talk a lot. "Anyways, I'll deal with Mikhail. Just be nice tonight. Okay?"

"When aren't I nice?"

She chuckles at my remark. It wasn't intended to be funny, but I'm not the most friendly and open guy.

Madisyn purses her lips, her cheeks rosy. "Just be civil. And you should join us for dinner."

Is she out of her mind? "Is this a setup?" I ask.

"What are you talking about?" Madisyn plays coy. She doesn't strike me for being stupid, and she didn't weasel her way into Mikhail's life based on luck. The girl is downright cunning. And while she left the bureau to pursue her full-time responsibilities at Steele Concierge Medical, I can't help but watch my back.

She betrayed Mikhail once. What's to say that she won't do it again?

"Hannah's involved with the guy I met last night. I don't know what you think you're doing, Madisyn, but stop."

Hannah has her life together. She's got a kid, a family, and she doesn't need me meddling in her personal affairs. I can fantasize about what we did, but that's as far as it can go. I'm not breaking apart her family or ruining her life for my selfish desires.

I'm not that much of a bastard.

"She's not married to him yet," Madisyn says.

I'm not breaking up their engagement because I had a fling with her a few years ago. "Are you out of your mind?"

"Fine, I'll leave it alone. But you should join us for dinner. Mikhail will appreciate your company."

———

"I'd like a word with you in my office," Mikhail says.

I head into the office and shut the door behind myself. "Everything all right, boss?" His hands are folded in front of him. The expression on his face is sour.

"Madisyn invited one of her colleagues from the clinic over for dinner."

He sounds about as happy as I feel over the ordeal. "Nikita already ran a background check on her friends and close colleagues."

"Yes, and I'm sure everything will be fine, but I'd like you to watch this girl coming for dinner. If she gets up to pee, I want you to follow her. I don't need another agent trying to weasel her way into my home."

I try to hide the smirk on my face.

"Is something funny, Luka?"

"No, sir." I know better than to piss the man off. He's given me a great deal of responsibility and trusts me. The last thing I want is to fuck that up over some girl.

"Madisyn mentioned that she might be bringing her child along. Make sure that the toys in the attic are brought down."

"Yes, sir." I'm surprised that the toys from his niece and nephew having lived with him are still under his roof. I'd have thought that he'd have torched them much like the relationship with his younger sister.

And while Mikhail had the playroom converted to an additional workspace, no one has dared use the space.

"I don't intend on them staying much past dinner, but Madisyn will insist on dessert, and it's unlikely a small child will have the patience to sit still for several hours," Mikhail says.

"I'll take care of it," I say before exiting Mikhail's office.

Within the hour, the doorbell chimes, and I answer it since I'm nearest to the door. Madisyn is hurrying down the stairs when I pull open the door.

Sure enough, Hannah brought her daughter along. The kid could be a mini version of Hannah, with the same hair and matching baby blue eyes.

"Mama, I'm cold," the little girl announces rather loudly as they stand at the front door.

"Come in," I say, forgetting my manners. I'm not used to guests showing up at the compound. We rarely have visitors who aren't members of the bratva.

Hannah helps the little girl out of her purple coat, and I offer to take it, hanging it in the nearby hall closet. She unlaces the toddler's boots while the child drops her hat and gloves on the floor.

I bend down to retrieve the items just as Hannah bends down, knocking into one another.

"Sorry," she says, quick to apologize as she reaches for the abandoned clothes, stuffing the items into her jacket pocket.

"It was my doing," I say. I'm not used to apologizing. It's not something that we do as bratva, showing any weakness.

Hannah unbuttons her coat and removes her shoes, leaving them by the front door. She follows me to the closet to hang her jacket. "I wasn't sure you were coming to dinner," Hannah says. She tugs her bottom lip between her teeth.

Is she nervous? I can't fathom why she would be.

"Mama!" the little tyke tugs on her mother's hand, attempting to drag her to follow. The kid isn't shy or nervous around strangers, let alone in new places.

"Bay, come here." Hannah bends down and sweeps the little tiger into her arms, not letting her roam free.

"She looks just like you," I say. The resemblance is uncanny.

Bay squirms in her mother's grasp, clearly wanting to be put down.

Madisyn strolls up from behind me. "Really? I'd say she looks remarkably like her father."

Hannah's eyes widen, and she glares at Madisyn. I'm not sure what's going on, but I let it slide. There's no logical reason that I don't like the guy from yesterday at Hannah's apartment.

Blame it on jealousy, but I don't want to talk about him with Hannah or Madisyn, for that matter.

I'd just assume that he doesn't exist.

Can't a guy pretend?

"You look like hell. What happened?" Madisyn asks, directing her question at Hannah.

"I don't want to talk about it," she says.

"Mean Mark," Bay proclaims, not the least bit privy that Hannah doesn't want to discuss the matter.

My hands bunch into fists at my side. There's a distant look in Hannah's eyes that I should have seen earlier. Her eyes are puffy and red. "How was he mean?" I growl. I'll kill him if he laid a finger on Hannah or Bay.

"Can I give you a bear hug?" Madisyn asks, holding out her arms to Bay.

The little girl's face brightens, and she nods vigorously as she squirms and wiggles to break free from her mother. Hannah relinquishes Bay into Madisyn's arms.

Madisyn steals Bay away, taking her down the hallway toward the kitchen.

Hannah rolls her lips together, her brow furrowing like she's trying not to cry. "We got into a fight."

I can't help but worry and wonder if he hurt Hannah. She's wearing a turtleneck, making it nearly impossible to see any skin.

I don't want to jump to conclusions, but she's still visibly shaken from whatever transpired.

I let her talk. The best thing that I can do right now is listen to her.

Hannah glances away, avoiding my heated stare. "It's stupid." She's quick to dismiss the argument, or at the very least, the discussion regarding whatever heated fight transpired earlier.

I want her to confide in me, if only so that she's happier and feels better. "Nothing you say is stupid." I step closer and bring my hand up to her chin.

She freezes. Her body tenses at the gesture. "Was he physical with you?" Anger surfaces at the thought that he did something to hurt her. The room is warm, and my adrenaline spikes. "Was he violent?"

I fear the answer that she'll give me. She has no visible scars, but the deeper cuts beneath the surface have me just as worried, and not only for Hannah, but for Bay.

She opens her mouth, and her voice is hardly above a whisper. Like she's afraid to say the words aloud. "He wouldn't let me leave."

"Intimidation." I pull her closer, my hands on her arms, examining her face and what I can see of her neck, looking for signs of physical abuse.

"No, it's more than that." Hannah grimaces.

Does she regret telling me the truth?

"How about we find someplace a little more comfortable and private to talk," I suggest as I walk with her down the hallway in the direction that Madisyn took Bay. I lead her into the study. It's empty, and I flip on the light as I step into the room.

Hannah follows close behind.

Laughter emanates from the dining room. Madisyn seems to be doing a decent job of entertaining the tiny tiger, which must put Hannah's mind at ease.

Her shoulders relax as she steps farther into the study and grabs a seat on the sofa.

I don't sit. I'm too restless and full of pent-up energy to unwind on the couch.

"Mark and I got into a pretty heated fight last night," Hannah says. Her hands are clasped in front of her. She gnaws on her bottom lip.

I stop pacing and stand a few feet away, pinning her with my stare. "And?" She's leaving something out of her story.

"It was about you," she says.

I take a step backward, surprised by her remark. "Let me guess, he's jealous and concerned because I drove you home?" I'm taking a stab at what the problem might be.

Does he think that she's cheating on him? Is that why they were fighting?

Sitting up, she gestures for me to come and join her on the couch.

I oblige and sit beside her, waiting for her to elaborate on what happened.

"It's about Bay," Hannah says.

"Bay? What does your daughter have to do with any of this? Was he upset that you didn't come home after work?" I'm trying to unravel what happened last night, and she's not exactly giving me the whole story.

Why is that?

What is she hiding?

I sit down on the sofa beside her, and she reaches for my hands.

"Mama! Mama! Mama!" Bay runs into the study. "Potty!" she squeals.

"Sorry!" Madisyn apologizes as she chases after Bay.

"I'll show her where the bathroom is," Madisyn says. "Come on." She holds out her hand for Bay to take.

Bay doesn't budge from her spot right in front of Hannah.

"It's fine. I'll take her. Can you just point me in the right direction," Hannah says as she stands and latches onto Bay's hand.

"Yeah." I stand and lead Hannah and Bay out into the hallway. We make a quick right and the second door on the left is the bathroom. I open the door and flip on the light for Bay.

"Mama," Bay says, pulling Hannah into the bathroom with her.

"Thank you," Hannah says and closes the door.

I glance around. The compound is relatively sparse for a Saturday night. Nikita and Anton went out for drinks. This means they're chasing a hot piece of ass tonight.

I'd be out with them if Hannah hadn't come over for dinner. Maybe I should have the night off and clear my head. She's bound to land my ass in trouble.

"Hungry yet?" Madisyn stalks up from behind.

I didn't hear her coming. The girl is stealthy.

I turn around to face her but ignore her question. She isn't asking about food. Why does she think anything will happen between Hannah and me? What game is she playing?

"Why don't you check on dinner and see if they're ready for us in the dining room?" I ask, trying to get Madisyn out of my hair.

Mikhail gave me orders to keep an eye on Hannah. Madisyn, however, is *his* responsibility. I still don't completely trust her, given that she used to work for the FBI. Who's to say she won't betray us?

She's proven herself loyal to Mikhail, which should be good enough for me. But I have my reservations, and I keep them to myself—no sense in upsetting the pakhan.

"I can wait for Hannah," Madisyn says.

"Mikhail instructed that I keep an eye on her." His orders aren't a secret, not in terms of the security and safety of his men. Madisyn should know that by now.

"Fine," she says and expels a heavy sigh as she sulks across the hall for the dining room.

Hannah unlatches the bathroom door, and Bay hurries out, running past me.

"Sorry," Hannah says. She's quick to apologize as she chases after the little girl and picks her up, keeping her from running rampant.

I lead her into the dining room. Mikhail and Madisyn are getting situated at the table, opening a bottle of wine and pouring the adults a glass.

"I'm sorry," Hannah apologizes. "Bay isn't usually this rambunctious."

Mikhail forces a smile. He never was particularly close with his niece and nephew when they lived under his roof. The mere thought of him raising a child, becoming a father, isn't something that I'd ever thought I'd witness.

And while I haven't seen it yet, Madisyn is pregnant. Eventually, she will have the child, and I can only imagine how Mikhail will handle the situation.

I run a hand through my hair, not wanting to dwell on a terse memory in present company.

"She's probably just hungry," I say and lift a piece of bread from the basket on the table. The staff brings out our meals, but Bay won't make it much longer without melting down. "May I?" I ask, checking with Hannah before handing the bread roll to Bay.

Hannah gives a brief nod, and Bay snatches the roll as though her life depends on it. That seems to do the trick as she focuses on eating.

"Have a seat," I say, helping Bay to the table, and Hannah grabs the seat next to her. I'm situated between Hannah and Mikhail. However, most of Mikhail's attention seems to be directed at Madisyn.

Glancing at Hannah, her hand comes up to her wine glass, her diamond engagement band glints under the candelabra. How had I missed that rock last night at the bar?

Was she wearing it last night?

I'm not the only one to notice it.

"Madisyn tells me that you're getting married," Mikhail says. "Have you picked out a venue?"

I reach for my glass of wine, needing something to keep me from cringing. I smile, hoping that she doesn't see through the charade.

Her brow furrows, and she presses her lips together. "Honestly, I don't know."

Dinner is served, and Hannah helps Bay with her meal, cutting it up but letting the little tiger feed herself.

I clear my throat, the wine glass in my hand, swirling the dark purple liquid. We should steer the conversation away from her fiancé and her upcoming nuptials. Hannah doesn't want to discuss it, and I'm not sure I want to hear it over dinner. I'll likely lose my appetite.

"How long have you been working at Steel Concierge Medical?" I ask, glancing at Hannah.

She expels a soft sigh, and her shoulders relax. "I've been with the company for seven years. What about you? Madisyn never told me what either of you does?" Hannah takes a small bite of dinner. She's mostly pushing the food around on her plate and keeping a watchful gaze on Bay.

While Madisyn knows that we're bratva, very few people who aren't part of our organization are aware of our business dealings.

"We buy and sell commodities," Mikhail says, quick to answer before I can respond.

"Oh, so you guys are like stock market brokers?" Hannah asks, giving him her undivided attention.

Madisyn takes a massive bite of her bread and glances away, trying to distract herself. I swear she's trying to keep from laughing. But shoving more food into her mouth doesn't seem like the best idea.

How the hell was she an FBI agent?

"Something like that," I say, glancing at Hannah.

The blue-eyed brunette is innocent; she has no idea what we do, and that's for the best. I doubt she'd have brought Bay with her if she realized that we're murderers.

We're not cold-blooded killers. Everyone I've ever killed, it was justified. They betrayed the family.

EIGHT

Hannah

Dinner goes better than I expect, given the fact that Bay wants to run around and explore every room of the mansion.

Mikhail excuses himself after dinner and kisses Madisyn before hightailing it out of the dining room. He's like a man on a mission. Does he work all hours of the night? Is that how he's able to afford such a luxurious home?

"Come on, let's have some girl time," Madisyn says.

My stomach is tangled in knots. She's going to want to know if I've told Luka about Bay.

I haven't.

He's much too warm and kind. I'm afraid of how he'll respond. I don't want Mark to be correct, that telling Luka is a mistake, but his words keep floating through my mind, replaying like a movie on repeat.

I follow Madisyn into the study, carrying a squirmy Bay.

"It was nice seeing you," I say to Luka.

I should tell him the truth. He deserves to hear it from me.

"Don't think that you're done with me yet."

What does he mean? Did Madisyn tell him about Bay?

I'm glad I didn't eat much for dinner because I wouldn't be able to keep it down. He disappears down the hallway, and I step into the study with Madisyn.

She flips on the lights and gestures for us to have a seat on the sofa.

"Down," Bay grumbles at me, squirming to be set free.

I put her feet on the ground, and she hurries to the window, staring outside into the darkened night. There isn't much to see, but it's captured her attention, which is good enough for me.

I plop down on the sofa, and Madisyn joins me. "Have you told him?"

"Mark doesn't want me to say anything. We got into a nasty fight last night, and it didn't get any better after work."

"Was it physical?" Madisyn asks. Her expression is grim as she glances me over from head to toe.

"I appreciate your concern, but I can handle Mark."

Luka clears his throat as he stands in the open doorway, carrying a box. "I brought some toys down from the attic. Bay might like to play with them," Luka says.

Bay's eyes light up, and she bolts toward Luka as he bends down, putting the cardboard box on the floor.

She digs her tiny hands into the box, pulling out a plastic police cruiser and fire truck.

"What do you say?" I ask Bay.

"Thank you," Bay answers, barely acknowledging Luka, her attention on the plastic vehicles rolling across the wooden floorboards.

"You're welcome," Luka says and quirks a sideways grin. "I'll give you two some privacy," he says and heads out of the study, closing the pocket door behind himself.

I wait until he's gone, and I'm confident that he's not on the opposite side of the door eavesdropping. Although if he were, it might make telling him easier.

"Mark is pissed at me about coming tonight, Luka being here, and me wanting to tell him the truth."

Madisyn pulls her legs up onto the sofa and sits facing me. "It's not up to Mark."

"I know that, but we're getting married. The last thing I want is to be fighting with him right now. I'm sure he's under a lot of stress with the wedding coming up."

"The wedding that he's leaving you to plan?" The blonde rolls her lips together. "I've tried to keep my opinion to myself, but maybe you should reconsider spending the rest of your life with him."

"Madisyn!" I can't believe her suggestion.

"Do you love him?" Madisyn asks, getting right to the point.

I did love him when he proposed. At least, I thought it was love, but the more time we spend together, the more I feel like I'm settling.

I avoid her question, but that's an answer in itself. "If I tell Luka the truth, Mark may never forgive me."

"You can't keep this a secret from Luka. You have to tell him the truth." Madisyn's eyes tighten as she glances from me to Bay. "If you don't tell him, I will."

"I plan to tell him. I just—I'm not sure what will happen at home."

"You need to do what's best for Bay," Madisyn says.

She's right. I know she's right. And I've convinced myself to tell Luka, but Mark has managed to tear me down and reconsider everything I thought I knew and wanted to do.

"I'll watch Bay if you want to talk with Luka."

My mouth is dry, and my voice is hoarse. "Now?"

"No time like the present," Madisyn says. Her brown eyes shine bright like she's enjoying my torment. "Just rip it off like a band-aid."

I exhale a nervous breath and stand. "Yeah, you're right." I came over tonight to talk to Luka about Bay. "Mark's going to be pissed," I mutter.

"Fuck him," Madisyn says, overhearing my remark.

I force a smile and head for the door. Bay doesn't even seem to notice that I'm leaving. She's enthralled by the new toys that Luka brought in for her to play with. Hopefully, she won't be too much of a handful for Madisyn.

When I slide the pocket door open, Luka stands across the hallway, his back leaning up against the wall, focusing on his phone.

He glances up the moment I open the door, and he shoves his phone into his pocket. "Need something?" Luka asks.

"Actually, yes. I wanted to talk with you, alone." I fiddle with my hands, anxiously playing with my fingers, unable to release the nervous energy pent up inside.

Luka glances past me at the study that Madisyn and Bay are occupying. "How about we find someplace private?" he suggests. He gently grabs my arm, and I wince.

I don't mean to, but there's probably a bruise left earlier in the evening by Mark. It didn't hurt until Luka touched it.

His brow furrows, and he opens a door, flips on the light, and gestures for me to step inside. It's an office with a deep mahogany desk in the center, black filing cabinets against the wall, and a closet door behind the desk, with a lock on the outside. There's a leather sofa against the wall.

He closes the door behind me. There are no windows, and no one can hear our conversation with the door shut.

I exhale a heavy breath. My stomach rumbles, and I can't quite calm my nerves.

"Is this about Mark?" Luka asks. His voice is kind and gentle, tender. He steps closer, his hand coming up to brush a strand of hair behind my ear.

"It's about Bay," I say.

The corners of his lips frown. "Is she all right?" Worry laces his tone as he leans back on the edge of his desk, supporting his weight. "She seems like she was enjoying herself tonight. Is she—unwell?"

I breathe a sigh of relief. Thankfully, Bay is healthy. "Bay is fine. She's your daughter," I blurt before I can stop myself. I imagined telling him how I had tried to reach out to him, find him, track him down, but I didn't know where he lived, worked, or even his last name.

"What?" Luka's eyes widen like he's just been slapped in the face.

"When we—that night several years earlier. She's the result," I say. It's not very eloquent, but it does the job.

"And you're just telling me now?" He backs away from the desk. The office is small, but he manages to pace the length from behind the desk, keeping adequate space from me. Luka loosens his tie first.

The small space is rather stuffy. He's not the only one feeling hot and trapped.

"I went back to the bar where we met, where I thought you might have worked. No one knew who you were. And the phone number that you left on a napkin got ruined by a glass of water." I certainly never thought that I'd need to keep his number or that we'd ever see each other again.

Luka exhales a sharp breath. His expression is grim. "Why now?"

"Why not?" I pin him with my stare. "Madisyn saw the picture on my phone. She told me she knew you, that you work for her boyfriend. I didn't expect you to be at the bar last night."

"You should have told me yesterday."

"That's not a conversation you spring on someone," I say.

Luka runs a hand through his short, jet-black hair. "I suppose there's never a good time to drop that bomb on someone."

He takes the news better than I'd expect.

He's silent, and I can see the cogs working in his head. He removes his suit coat and hangs it over the office chair. The calmness he exudes quickly evaporates. "All through dinner, you just sat there and led me to believe that she's someone else's kid." His tone rises as he speaks.

"I'm telling you now." I step backward, knocking into the door, the knob digging into my back.

"Why?" Luka's question is gruff. "Do you want money? Is that why you're coming to me?"

"Of course not!" I reach behind me for the door handle and step forward just enough to open the door and slip out. "Mark was right. This was a mistake," I mutter, but I'm not particularly quiet with my remark.

"Get back here!" Luka shouts.

I don't listen to him. It's bad enough that I have to deal with Mark's temper tantrums. I don't have to be a part of Luka's outbursts too. I hurry down the hall and slip into the study, lifting Bay off the floor.

"Put down!" Bay wiggles and kicks her legs, squirming.

"It's time to go," I say, carrying her out into the hallway.

Madisyn leaps from the sofa. "What happened?" She chases after me as I head toward the front hall to retrieve our coats.

"I need to get home before turning into a pumpkin," I say. I retrieve my keys from my pocket and click the autostart button, letting the car heat up.

Madisyn is right behind me. She grabs Bay's boots and helps her into them while I open the coat closet.

Luka is on my heel. "We need to talk," Luka says, his jaw tight. He folds his arms across his chest. His biceps strain through his crisp white shirt.

He looks good out of his suitcoat, and my mind wanders to the two of us that night, my body wrapped around his, my back against the door, the fridge, everywhere but the bed.

I shouldn't even be thinking about sex with Luka Ivanov.

I'm engaged.

"I have to get home," I say and brush past him, retrieving Bay's coat. Bending down, I help her into her jacket before grabbing mine off the hanger. I slip on my boots, pull Bay's hat over her head, and slip on her gloves.

"Thank you for inviting us over for dinner," I say, giving Madisyn a quick hug goodbye.

"Of course. I'll see you at work tomorrow."

I pick Bay up and hurry outside.

Luka is right on my heel, following me down to the car. I unlock the back door with the keyless remote, and Luka opens it while I shuffle Bay into her car seat and get her situated.

"If you don't want money, why tell me about her?"

I shut the car door and shove my hands into my pocket. The air is icy, but it's not any more biting than Luka's mood.

"I thought you'd want to know that you have a kid, maybe even be a father to her." I thought that I was doing the right thing, allowing Luka to get to know Bay and for my daughter to have the chance to know her biological father.

Pinching the bridge of my nose, I lean back against the car door. "Listen, I don't want anything. It was a mistake coming here, telling you about

Bay. Just forget about it. Okay? You can go about your life, blissfully ignorant that you fathered a child."

Luka growls and leans in, his body trapping me against the cold metal of the car. "That's not fair. I didn't know about her until a few minutes ago."

He's close enough that I can feel his breath and shiver from his proximity.

"I deserve the chance to know Bay," he says.

I gently rest my hand on his chest and push him back, needing space between us. "We'll talk another day."

"When?"

I hadn't given it much thought.

"Do you work tomorrow?" he asks.

"Yes. But I have Monday off."

"Swing by Monday afternoon. Text me before you get here, and I'll make sure that I'm free and we can talk." He holds out his hand. "Your phone?"

I dig my cell phone out of my pocket and grimace at the half dozen missed calls and fourteen unread messages Mark left. He's never been exceptionally clingy, but my stomach roils.

"Someone is popular," he says, noticing the notifications on my screen.

"Yeah." I don't want to talk about it. Hell, I don't want to go home and deal with Mark, but I can't shove my head into the sand.

I hand Luka my phone, and he inputs his cell phone number. "Text me when you're on your way."

"Will do. It'll be after lunch, around one o'clock," I say.

"That's fine." He hands me my phone and leans in, his breath mixing with mine.

I inhale a sharp breath, and he grazes my cheek with his lips. "Stay safe," he whispers, his lips moving to my ear. "And if that boyfriend of yours lays a finger on you, I'll kill him."

NINE

Luka

The Next Day...

Nikita pokes his head into my office. "You've got a visitor," he says.

"I do?"

Hannah isn't supposed to come by until tomorrow. I step out from behind my desk and head into the hallway.

What is *she* doing here?

Hannah and Bay stand at the entryway by the front door, suitcase in hand. Hannah's shaking, and Bay is latched onto her mother's leg. I've never seen the little girl look quite so frightened. Yesterday, she was bubbly and expressive, wanting to explore every inch of the compound.

"Come on in," I say, kneeling as I help Bay out of her coat.

Hannah stands there, frozen.

Numb.

I'll kill whoever did this to her.

Hannah hasn't said a single word. Her bottom lip trembles, and I glance over my shoulder at Nikita. "Go find Madisyn."

His brow knits, but he follows my order, hurrying up the stairwell.

I remove Bay's hat and gloves along with her boots by the time Madisyn clomps down the stairs. "Oh my gosh!" Madisyn's voice carries through the hallway, and she rushes to the front door. "You weren't at work today."

"He wouldn't let me leave," Hannah whispers. Her voice cracks, and she's trying to keep herself together. I'd guess for Bay's sake.

"What?" Did I hear her correctly?

My blood boils, and I drop Bay's jacket on the floor in a daze. I bend down, picking the purple coat up off the floor.

The damn wedding had better be off.

There's no way in hell that I'm letting her leave and go back to him. Certainly not with my child. However, she's brought a suitcase. Maybe she intends to stay here. Hannah has barely said two words. Her bottom lip trembles, and the girl looks like she's in shock.

Mikhail won't be pleased if she intends to stay at the compound. I should talk to him before Madisyn does, explain the situation.

What the hell is the situation?

Hannah has barely said anything since she stepped foot inside. I glance past her out the window. There's no sign of her car.

How did she get here?

"Here," Madisyn says and takes Bay's coat from my hands. She brings the items to the hall closet, hangs her jacket up, and shoves the gloves into the pockets.

"Let me take your coat. You can stay for as long as you need." I'm not sure why I'm making such a generous offer without consulting Mikhail, but the words are out before I can recant them.

She's in trouble and needs my help.

Her lips part, but the words don't follow. She mouths a simple *thank you*.

She unbuttons her coat, and I guide her jacket off, noticing a discoloration around her neck. "Is that a bruise?"

Did the bastard lay a finger on her? My breathing grows louder and thicker as anger mounts to the surface.

Hannah lifts the collar of her shirt, but it does little to hide the mark left behind. Only a coward uses violence to intimidate and threaten a woman.

"I'll kill him." It's not an empty threat. I'll bury the asshole alive. Anyone who fucks with Hannah will have to get through me.

I whip my car keys from my pants pocket. There's no way in hell I'm going to sit around when he hurt Hannah.

He must pay for what he's done.

Hannah's pale blue eyes widen, and her breathing hitches.

Madisyn clears her throat and glares at me. "Don't even think about it."

What the hell did I do?

"Keep an eye on Bay, and I'll take Hannah upstairs and get her situated." Madisyn doesn't wait for me to answer. She gestures for Nikita to grab her friend's suitcase.

Nikita wordlessly retrieves her single piece of luggage and carries it upstairs.

Since when is Madisyn in charge?

"You want me to stay here and let the bastard who hit your friend get away with it?" That's not how I operate. He deserves to pay for his sins and I'm just the man to teach him a lesson.

"Please, no." Tears trickle down Hannah's cheek and the waterworks with Bay follow.

Hannah glances up at me, her bottom lip trembles, and tears well in her eyes. "Keep an eye on Bay."

How can I say no to her?

I bend down to Bay's level. "Hi," I say, offering an awkward smile. It's not like I haven't been around kids. Mikhail's sister had raised her twins the first few years in the compound until she was reunited with the father.

Bay wipes the tears from her face with the back of her hand. "I remember you," she says.

I would hope so, I'd just had dinner with the kid and with Hannah, yesterday.

The little girl continues to stare at me with wide eyes and sniffles.

"Good," I say and exhale a sigh. "How about we find you a tissue?"

Bay nods vigorously, and that's good enough for me. At least the kid isn't fighting me, begging to be at her mother's side.

Madisyn takes Hannah's hand and guides her up the stairwell as I lead Bay into the study while she's momentarily distracted.

The box of toys is situated against the wall, and Bay runs toward them, pulling out the plastic vehicles and plopping herself down on the ground.

I grab the box of tissues from the nearby table and bring one to Bay, handing it to her.

She lifts her head at me and waits. Hannah must dote on the kid.

"Here." I hand the tissue to Bay, and she pats her eyes, likely mimicking what her mother does for her.

When she's finished, I toss it in the trash and sit on the nearby sofa. Bay isn't particularly chatty tonight. Is it because of what happened at the apartment?

Did she witness what transpired between Hannah and her fiancé?

I swallow the lump in my throat.

Did he lay a finger on Bay?

She doesn't appear physically unwell. Emotionally, I can't say.

"Which truck is your favorite?" I ask as she slams the fire engine into the police cruiser.

That's my girl, causing chaos.

My stomach tenses at my inward admission and thoughts, *my girl*. She is my daughter. I crouch down, and she hands me the police cruiser.

Not my first choice, but I'm not going to argue with Bay. I don't want to see her cry again, and at least the last time wasn't my doing.

"Thanks." I force a smile.

"Sit," she orders and points at the ground.

I flop onto my ass unceremoniously as I join her on the floor. Bay plows her fire engine into my police cruiser.

"Daddy says we have to move."

"Daddy?" I repeat, confused by her remark. She lifts the fire engine into the air as though it were capable of flight and drops it to the ground.

"I don't want to move to Cannon."

Cannon? Where the fuck is that? Does Hannah want to move? Is she planning on taking Bay?

The study is warm, and the air feels sucked right out of my lungs. I can't pretend to sit here and play any longer. "Stay here," I demand and place the police cruiser on the floor beside Bay.

I stand and hurry out of the room, closing the pocket door. I breeze past Nikita. "Stay outside the study, and make sure Bay doesn't leave." I point down the hall at the closed door to the study.

"Will do," he says and heads in the direction of where I just came from. I head to the stairwell and take the steps two at a time.

I suspect Hannah is in the empty bedroom next to Madisyn, but there are quite a few unoccupied rooms on the second floor and a half dozen more on the third.

The bedroom is shut, but I can hear muffled voices on the opposite side. I give a hefty knock before yanking the door open.

Hannah is seated on the bed, and Madisyn is next to her. Hannah's been crying. Her eyes are red and swollen, and she wipes the last remnants of tears away as though she could hide her pain from me.

"I asked you to keep an eye on Bay," Hannah says. She glances past me. Is she expecting that I brought her upstairs?

"She's in the study with a handful of toys. She's fine. I have Nikita keeping an eye on the door if she wanders out looking for you."

Hannah presses her lips together and nods. She exhales a heavy breath through her nose, and I think she might be done crying.

"Bay mentioned that you're moving."

She tugs her bottom lip between her teeth, gnawing nervously—her gaze glances to Madisyn.

"Would you like me to give you both a minute?" Madisyn asks Hannah.

Hannah's shoulders slouch, her hands are nestled in her lap. "Yeah, if you would. Can you check on Bay?"

"Of course, I'll keep her company." Madisyn hugs Hannah before climbing off the edge of the bed and stalking past me as she heads for the door. "She's vulnerable. Don't you dare hurt her," Madisyn threatens in my ear on her way out of the room.

I wouldn't dream of it. She's not the one who deserves my wrath.

That asshole of a fiancé, I hope I can refer to him as her ex-fiancé. He doesn't deserve her.

Madisyn quietly exits the bedroom and closes the door behind herself, leaving us alone.

"Where the hell is Cannon?" I ask, folding my arms across my chest. Is she planning on skipping town to get away from that bastard?

Her brow tightens, and her nose crinkles at my question. "What?"

It's almost cute if I weren't growing irritated that she's considering leaving New York and has no intention of telling me the truth. "I had to hear it from Bay that you're moving."

Hannah's eyes light up as she understands what I'm asking. "The Cayman Islands."

"You're moving?"

Fuck.

"No, I mean I don't want to." Hannah drops her head into her hands, her face down toward her lap. "Mark insists that we're moving to the Caymans when we get married."

"You're still planning on marrying him?"

I sit next to Hannah on the bed, my legs brushing against hers as the bed dips.

"No, but I haven't exactly broken it off with him yet, either. I snuck out with Bay when he went to take a shower." Her voice cracks, and I wrap my arm around her shoulders.

Instantly, she leans her head into my shoulder and emits a sharp gasp like she's trying not to cry. "Whatever you need, I'm here."

I want to pound that asshole's head into the pavement, but I don't imagine Hannah will appreciate the gesture. Although it might be worth her disapproving stare, I don't want to frighten her.

"Thank you," Hannah says and emits a heavy sigh.

She rests a hand on my thigh, and my cock twitches in my trousers. Just one touch, and my body responds, eager to please her, but that isn't what she wants or needs from me. I rest my hand on hers, resting her palm back on her lap.

It's the adrenaline and her scent pumping hormones into the air. I clear my throat and stand, needing to clear my head before I do something stupid, like kiss her.

That's the last thing she wants from me. "You've done well raising Bay," I say, attempting to change the subject.

Her gaze rises to meet my heated stare.

"I want to be involved in her life." I don't know what Hannah was expecting when she told me that I'm Bay's father, but if it's true, I can't just ignore that I have a kid.

"Of course. I assume you'll want to take a paternity test," Hannah says. "Although, there's no one else it could be." She glances away, her cheeks redden.

Is she blushing?

I want to verify that Bay is my flesh and blood, but that isn't something we have to do right this second.

Standing just a few feet away, I fold my arms across my chest. "Do you want to talk about what that bastard did to you? Because the way I see it, you ought to be either pressing charges or letting me go pound the shit out of him."

The corner of her lip turns upwards. Does she think I'm joking? I'd gladly bloody the asshole who hurt her. It's not like I don't know where he lives. "The cops won't do much."

"He left that bruise," I say and gesture toward her neck. "Did he leave any other marks?"

She raises the collar on her shirt, but it doesn't help. Does she think she can hide what he did to her from me? "It was an accident."

"No." I close the distance between us. "Don't excuse his actions. He knew what he was doing. You said so yourself. He trapped you. He didn't let you go into work this morning."

"Mark was angry with me. He insisted that I keep Bay a secret from you. That's what the fight was about. It escalated when he told me that it doesn't matter; we're all moving to the Caymans after the wedding."

I hate this guy even more. I didn't think that would be possible. "He deserves to get his face bashed in."

Hannah smiles weakly. "That may be true, but you don't have to defend my honor."

"Is the wedding off?" I need to hear from her lips that she isn't going back to him.

"I want him out of my house. Will you and Madisyn come with me when we tell him to leave?"

Madisyn and Hannah have no business being anywhere near Mark. "Mikhail and I will take care of it." If Mikhail is busy, I can bring one of our soldiers to accompany me. "Does he know where you're staying?"

Her tongue darts out, swiping across her lips. "I'm sure he'll figure out I'm with Madisyn, but he doesn't know the address, and I left my car at the apartment complex."

"How did you get here?"

"I grabbed a cab outside the building. I thought it would be safer than driving my car if Mark tried to track my vehicle."

Good, then we won't have to worry about ditching her car or checking it for a tracking device. I glance at my watch. Mikhail and I could go tonight, rough Mark up, and tell him to leave the apartment, but I still wouldn't feel comfortable about Hannah and Bay returning home even if we change the locks.

"Stay here tonight. I'll talk to Mikhail, and we'll swing by and have a word with Mark tomorrow. Do you have work in the morning?"

"No, I'm supposed to have off, but I didn't exactly show up this morning to work."

"We'll deal with that tomorrow. Jot down where Mark works, any other places that he frequents, and if you know the details of his schedule."

Hannah chuckles at my thoroughness. "What are you scheduling, a hit on his ass? You're worse than Madisyn. I don't know the place he works; it's an accounting firm. I've never been to his office."

"Just write down whatever you know."

She has no idea what I'm capable of doing. But I doubt Hannah would agree to Mikhail or myself executing the bastard. Besides, I'd rather rough him up and put fear into him.

"Tomorrow is Monday," I say, reminding her that it's a workday for most people. "I would assume that he has to go into the office. It'd be less convenient for him if we showed up at his work. I want the address of his office and his hours."

"You want to humiliate him?" Her hand trembles as she rests it on her lap.

"I just want to clarify that he is to leave you alone and get his stuff and go."

Will Hannah feel safe returning to her apartment even after Mark leaves? I'm not keen on her returning unless one of our men is stationed outside of her door, keeping a close eye on the two of them indefinitely.

"Seems fair," Hannah says. She stands and wipes the last remnants of any remaining tears away, stalking toward me.

"Should we go downstairs and see how Bay is doing? Have you two eaten anything tonight?" I ask.

"I gave Bay some snacks, so she probably won't be hungry for dinner, and I don't have much appetite." She opens the bedroom door, and I follow out into the hallway behind her. "So, you're over at Madisyn's place quite a bit."

"Mikhail's place," I correct her.

"Right," she says. Hannah glances at me as we crest the staircase, awaiting my response. "So?"

How do I tell her I live here, upstairs, without her growing suspicious of what we do for a living?

What ordinary man has a half dozen grown men living with him, and it isn't a frat house? Even billionaires have security, but they go home when another shift arrives at the end of the night.

Mikhail isn't a billionaire, but he runs an empire, and I work for him, guarding our home and brothers.

I avoid her question. It's easier to distract her and shift the topic to anything else. "He's always got a stocked fridge," I joke and head down the stairs, letting her follow behind me. "I assume your accommodations are to your liking."

"You're evasive, and I like how you just change the subject on a whim. And yes, I'm appreciative of the space for Bay and me to share. I'll have to thank Mikhail personally."

She catches up alongside me as I willfully stride into the study. The sooner I'm in Madisyn and Bay's presence, the fewer questions I'll face from Hannah.

"Mama!" Bay glances up from her fire engine and drops the toy with an unceremonious thud to the floor.

Hannah hurries across the room and bends down, hugging Bay. "Are you having fun with your new toys?"

Bay nods vigorously. "It's time to get ready for bed," Hannah says. "Can you clean up your toys?"

Madisyn pulls me aside while Hannah helps Bay put the toys that she pulled out back into the box.

"What's up?" I ask.

"Mark has been calling and texting non-stop."

I'm not surprised, considering how she left and his behavior. He's probably begging Hannah to come home, promising he'll never hurt her again.

Madisyn pulls out a cell phone from her pocket. "It's Hannah's. She asked me to hold on to it. She was worried she'd do something stupid."

"It's still on?" I snatch the phone from Madisyn's grasp and head out into the hallway, removing the sim card.

How could she not have thought to turn it off? He could be tracking her!

"We've got company," Mikhail's gruff voice carries through the hallway.

I close the pocket door of the study, keeping them out of whatever drama is about to ensue. "Do we know who it is?"

"I'd guess Hannah's ex. Nikita mentioned that Hannah came by unexpectedly. The asshole is probably looking for his kid."

"Bay isn't his kid." I won't elaborate.

I march up to the window and glance out past the open curtains. It's difficult to see much in the dark, but there's a vehicle with headlights shining straight at us on the opposite side of the gate.

"Who is watching the gate?" I ask, wanting to know who is posted tonight at the entrance, watching the compound.

"Anton."

I exhale a heavy breath and pinch the bridge of my nose.

"Yeah, my thoughts exactly," Mikhail says. "If I had realized Madisyn brought drama home, I'd have given Anton back up at the entrance."

"You're worried about Mark getting through the front gate?" I never expected that Mikhail would have grievances against Anton. He's a loyal but young soldier. He doesn't have much world experience, especially in terms of bloodshed.

I'm not suggesting Anton slaughter Mark, although it would save me from tomorrow's drama.

"I'm worried about having to replace the gate. He sounds feeble-minded and may drive through the front entrance, not caring that the entry is shut. How the hell did he even manage to track them down?"

"Hannah's phone was turned on. I removed the sim card just a moment ago."

Mikhail isn't one to back down from a fight.

Neither am I.

TEN

Luka

Mikhail opens the front door, and I accompany him outside.

Mark is parked just on the opposite side of the gate, headlights on, beaming at the compound.

"We'll get rid of him," I say.

Anton is standing outside of the security booth, speaking with Mark on the driver's side of the black four-door truck.

Mark revs the engine. "I want to talk to Hannah!" he shouts. His window is rolled down and he wallops the side of his truck with his hand.

"She'd better be worth it," Mikhail mutters under his breath.

I can't hear Anton's response from across the yard, and I don't answer Mikhail. My sidearm is loaded and ready if I need to use it or threaten the bastard.

I stroll up ahead of Mikhail, standing on the opposite side of the metal gate. We're not opening the door to this low life. He doesn't get to come anywhere near Hannah or Bay.

And while I intended to show up at his office tomorrow, I may as well give him the *leave her the fuck alone* speech that I intended to do.

A smaller gate beside the booth requires a code to enter and exit the premises. I punch in the six-digit code and step outside.

Mikhail follows and yanks the gate shut.

Over my dead body, is Mark getting inside or anywhere near Hannah and my daughter.

"Do you think it's fine to go around and assault women?" I shout as I stomp closer toward the pickup, my strides long and fast as I approach the vehicle.

Mark thrusts the door open.

Does he think he has a shot in hell against me?

Anton steps aside, but he's armed and ready should the need arise. He's waiting for Mikhail or my order to subdue the man and bring him to his knees.

That would be easy.

But I'm not about doing things the easy way tonight.

Mark deserves to suffer for what he's done, for hurting Hannah.

I don't take kindly to abusers.

Mikhail is directly behind me. I can feel his presence without so much as looking over my shoulder.

He's letting me take the lead. Does he know why this means everything to me?

"I don't know what you're talking about." Mark plays dumb. It's probably not hard since he's an idiot, but that doesn't excuse what he did to Hannah or Bay. "Let me see my wife!"

He stumbles headfirst into me. Is he trying to fight me, because he has zero chance of winning, let alone getting in a decent shiner?

His breath wreaks of liquor. How the hell did he drive here and not kill himself?

I couldn't be that lucky.

I push him off and shove him up against his vehicle, my left hand gripping his shirt. He's not wearing a jacket and too drunk to notice that it's cold.

I'm fired up inside from him showing up and giving me the perfect punching bag.

"First of all, she's not your wife." Disgust fills me that he would even think to call her his wife like he takes pride and possession of her. She's not an object, and frankly, they're not married.

His words slur, but they're still somewhat comprehensible. "You must be Luka," Mark sneers at me.

A certain amount of pride fills me, the fact that he knows my name because of Hannah.

I let go of him. If he can't stand on his own, let his drunk ass hit the curb.

He wobbles for a moment and then straightens himself up.

I don't confirm my identity. It doesn't matter if he knows my name or not. What matters is that he leaves Hannah and Bay alone.

"Do you find enjoyment in threatening women?" I ask, pulling my gun from its holster and shoving the barrel up under his neck. "Do you like making Hannah feel like she can't leave? Do you honestly think that holding her hostage gives you power over her?"

His eyes are glassy, and he swats at my hands. Any sane man would cower with a cocked gun beneath their chin.

Mark isn't the least bit sane or sober. I'll credit his stupidity with being drunk and not realizing that he's fucking with the bratva.

He doesn't answer me. He opens his mouth, but he's rendered speechless or too drunk to form a coherent response. I'd like to think it's the former, but I suspect it's the alcohol raging through his system.

"You will leave Hannah alone. You're not to have any contact with her or her daughter. Is that clear?"

Mark huffs under his breath.

"What's that?" I shove the pistol farther up into his neck.

Mark swallows. "Crystal," he whispers, his voice high-pitched and squeaky.

Is he nervous?

Good. I want to make him quiver and piss himself. That's the nicest thing that I'd bestow on his sorry ass before shoving him back into his pickup.

Sweat glistens on his brow.

If the guy has a heart attack, I'm leaving him outside to die. It's the best thing I could do for Hannah.

"And that apartment that you've been residing in, *Hannah's apartment*," I say, emphasizing that it isn't his home. "You take your shit and get out. If you bother her or come anywhere near Bay, we will hunt you down and castrate you."

Mikhail comes to stand beside me. "Consider that the nicest thing we'd do to you," he adds.

"I want to hear it from Hannah," Mark says, although it comes out whinier and more pathetic than a threat.

I withdraw my gun from Mark's chin and point it at his crotch. "Your choice. Leave her alone, or I shoot off your dick. I'd be doing every woman in New York City a favor."

Mark holds up his hands, swaying a bit as he leans back against the pickup for support. "Fine. No girl is worth that amount of trouble."

I take a step back, only enough that Mark can climb back into his truck and get himself killed on the way home. A guy can dream, right?

ELEVEN

Hannah

I head out of the study with Bay in my arms, ready to take her upstairs and tuck her into bed. One of the taller gentlemen in a suit stands by the window, focusing on something transpiring outside.

"What's going on?" I ask.

There's no sign of Luka. Where did he disappear to?

Madisyn comes up from behind and glances out the window. "Nikita has it covered. You should tuck Bay into bed." She whisks me away from the front hall and to the staircase.

It's Mark.

He must be outside, demanding that I come home.

My hands tremble, and I hug Bay tighter to my chest as I hurry up the stairs.

Madisyn is right on my heel. "Come on," she says, ushering us upstairs and hidden from view. At least, I assume that's her plan if Mark ends up inside.

Luka won't let him inside the house. He'd protect Bay, wouldn't he?

"How'd he find us?" I ask.

Madisyn shakes her head, not answering my question, her gaze on Bay. She pats her back and steps around me, opening the bedroom door. "Goodnight, Bay," Madisyn says, giving her the biggest reassuring smile.

My stomach flops.

I wish I could feel safe and calm and reassure Bay that everything is fine. Madisyn closes the bedroom door behind us, and I get Bay changed into her pajamas. I didn't bring too many clothes or belongings. I'd quickly shoved as much of Bay's clothes into one piece of luggage and a handful of my clothes to wear. It was risky packing while Mark was in the shower.

I still have access to my bank account. Thankfully, we aren't married yet. But I'm not sure if I still have my job after not showing up this morning.

I'll deal with it tomorrow.

I pull back the covers, and Bay climbs under the sheets. "Bunny," she says.

I grab her stuffed animal from the luggage. She's slept with her favorite toy since she was born. There was no chance of leaving it behind and risking a meltdown. At least I had enough forethought to grab it when I packed.

"Mama." Bay gestures for me to come closer, and I tuck her in and give her lots of hugs and kisses before shutting off the lights and heading quietly out of the bedroom.

It may be Bay's bedtime, but it's not mine. I'm exhausted, but I doubt that I'd get any sleep.

Madisyn stands in the hallway, her back against the wall.

I didn't expect her to wait for me. I head for the top of the stairs, away from the bedroom door, so that Bay can't overhear us. I want her to get some sleep, and the last thing she needs is for the grownups to be keeping her awake.

"Is it really Mark downstairs?" I ask.

"Outside," Madisyn corrects me. "He's not in the house. You can relax, Mikhail isn't going to invite him inside, and there's no way he's getting through his army."

"Army?" I suppose she's trying to make me feel better. I pull Madisyn in for a hug. "Thank you. I appreciate everything that you're doing for me. You're an amazing friend."

"I know," Madisyn quips with a wide grin. "Don't worry. I'm not going to let Mark get anywhere near you or Bay. And I'm confident Mikhail and Luka are doing the same thing. Trust me when I say this place is a fortress."

My bottom lip trembles as I stalk down the stairs. I'm grateful for the added security outside and the guard gate. It seems a bit like overkill—for what, exactly, I don't know, but I don't care right now.

The truth is that a small part of me wants to glance out the window and see what's going on, not that I expect to see much. It's dark outside, and if they're not right in front of the window, it's probably impossible to see anything.

But I should let Luka handle things with Mark, at least right now. I'm not ready to talk to him or deal with the last twenty-four hours until Mark is sober and I've had enough sleep to feel human again.

"Come on," Madisyn says and throws her arm around my shoulder. She guides me quickly past the window and into the kitchen.

"Wow." The place is enormous. I mean, I shouldn't be shocked considering the size of the house, but it's bigger than my apartment. Which, I suppose, isn't saying much. It's also immaculate. I'm guessing that Mikhail hires help, if not a chef. "Are you sure Mikhail isn't a billionaire?" I joke. Except, I'm curious how he affords his lavish lifestyle.

"You would think, with the way he has an entire staff to help him around here," Madisyn says. She opens the fridge and grabs a bag of grapes. Taking the fruit to the sink, she washes it before dropping the contents into a bowl and placing it on the counter. "Eat."

"I'm not hungry."

Madisyn stands at the opposite end of the counter. She grabs a grape and pops it into her mouth. "You're missing out."

How can she manage to eat right now? It's probably because it's not her crazy fiancé trying to break down the gate and drag her back home.

Heavy footsteps tromp through the hall. I shiver and glance over my shoulder as Luka struts into the kitchen.

"Your ex is an ass," Luka says. He doesn't sugarcoat what he thinks of the man.

"He's not normally like this," I say. I've never known Mark to behave in such a manner. He's always been sweet and, honestly, a bit bland. A definite workaholic but never aggressive or unkind until recently. It's almost like a switch has been flicked, and a mad man has awoken and taken over his mind and body.

"I hope you're not planning on going back to him." Luka's darkened gaze tightens as he glances me over. "You can do better than that low life." He steps around to stand beside me.

I exhale a loud sigh and lean forward on the counter, resting my elbows on the marble and my chin on my clasped hands. "It isn't that simple."

He clears his throat, and it's impossible not to notice the look that Madisyn gives Luka. "What?" I ask. They're having a private conversation with just a glance, and I'm not part of it.

Luka clears his throat again, and Madisyn is subtly shaking her head.

I drop my arms to my sides. "This is ridiculous! If you have something to say, just out with it," I say.

Luka invades my personal space. If he steps any closer, he'll be on my lap. His leg brushes against mine, and his fingers gently rake through my hair before he guides my chin up to meet his stare. "You're not going back to him." His voice is firm, and there's a finality in his command.

His touch sends a rippling pulse through my body, and my breathing deepens. It's subtle. At least I hope

Luka doesn't notice the effect that he has on me, the way my body willing responds to his demands.

Madisyn quietly retreats from the kitchen, leaving the two of us alone.

My heart hammers against my ribcage.

Luka hasn't released his grasp on my chin. His hand gently caresses my throat.

"You deserve better," Luka rasps, and his lips are close enough that I can feel his warm breath teasing me.

I want to kiss him, but everything inside me screams that it's too soon. We've gone down this road once, and it led to Bay. Everything that I do from this point onward must be for her.

His thumb gradually traces my bottom lip, and the desire builds inside me. Each shallow breath deepens. The kitchen is hot and stuffy, like a sauna, as I'm flooded with warmth.

"I should never have let you go," Luka whispers.

The warmth that spreads through me is unlike anything I've ever felt with Mark.

I lean closer and my lips part. I desperately ache to kiss Luka, pull him against me and feel anything but pain. "We can't," I whisper, my gaze unwavering.

I've managed to break the spell, and his hand gingerly falls while he takes a step back.

"You're right." He clears his throat and glances in the direction where Madisyn had been standing a few moments earlier.

Did he just realize that she'd left the two of us alone?

"I just got out of a relationship," I offer in the way of an explanation. It's not that I don't want to tangle in the sheets with Luka. It's that we can't do that if it's going to be a one-time thing.

Well, technically, twice.

"Good. That imbecile is no good for you," he says. His response is gruff. There's no smile on his face, but his eyes aren't cold.

"He wasn't very good in bed, either," I say and offer a wayward grin.

Luka chokes on his laughter. "I'm sorry." His face reddens as he's bent over, catching his breath.

He wasn't expecting my remark. It's the truth, and while maybe I should have kept that tidbit to myself, it just kind of slipped out.

"It's not that funny." I scowl and fold my arms across my chest.

He takes a deep breath, regaining his composure. "You're right, *Zaya*. It's not funny. A woman should enjoy every moment of being ravished."

"*Zaya*?" I tilt my head, curious about the name. Who is *Zaya*? "Are you sure you don't have a girlfriend or a wife hiding around here?" I joke, glancing over my shoulder, tripping over the leg of the counter stool when I take a step.

He catches me before I can make an ass out of myself and hit the floor.

His strong, rough hands steady me, and the distance built between us is gone.

Luka's hands are on my hips, and his touch sends butterflies to my stomach. His fingers caress my skin between the hem of my shirt and my pants. "No girlfriend or wife," he says. "And I hope you don't feel the same way about that night we shared."

I whimper from the caress of his touch. Like gravity, I'm pulled closer, our bodies practically touching. It takes everything to keep distance between us.

"It was a long time ago," I remind him. We're different people than when we first met.

"You mean to tell me that you don't remember that night?" Luka asks. He smiles and glances down, taking a long look at my clothed body, but I feel that he's remembering me naked. He leans closer. His breath caresses my ear. "He did you a favor, showing his true colors."

"What's that?" I ask, pulling back just slightly to meet his gaze.

He glances away with a smirk. "I shouldn't. You made it clear that you just want to be friends. And I need to respect that decision."

I've never regretted anything more in my life.

"We have a kid who needs to come first," I say. Bay is my highest priority. It's part of the reason that I had intended on marrying Mark, to give her a stable home. That plan backfired, but her needs are more important than my own.

Luka pushes a strand of hair behind my ear. His touch rekindles an old flame. "*Zaya*, you need to learn to put yourself first."

I press my lips together.

He smiles. "No witty comeback?" His touch is both soothing and stirs a fire inside of me.

"Agree to disagree," I say. If Luka thinks he can talk his way into my bed, he's mistaken.

His fingers caress my neck before he withdraws his hand. "You'll never be happy if you're chasing after what you think she needs."

I want to ensure that she has the best possible life. How is that wrong?

"She needs a stable home." He can't argue with that, and it's something that I didn't have growing up. I want to give her a better life than I had as a child.

"What about your needs?"

"I'd like to have a stable home, too," I smirk.

"Move in here, permanently," Luka says. There's no smile on his face. No laughter to indicate that he's joking.

He can't be serious.

My jaw drops at his request. "Think about what you're asking me to do. We don't even know each other."

"We knew each other enough to sleep together," Luka says. He reaches for my hand.

I swear if he's going to drop down onto one knee, I'll slug him.

"I want to be in Bay's life," Luka says. He squeezes my hand.

"And you will. But asking me to move in with you, that's a huge step." Doesn't he realize that moving in together is a monumental step?

"It doesn't have to be. I'll feel better knowing that you're not in that apartment. I made it known that Mark needs to leave you alone, but it'd be a lie if I said I thought he'd be smart and heed my advice."

"And Mikhail is okay with it?"

"You let me worry about him," Luka says. "Is that a yes?"

TWELVE

Luka

I don't know how I convinced Hannah to move in with me, but she agreed. Under the condition that Mikhail is willing to accept Hannah and Bay under his roof.

If I can prove to him that it's good for Madisyn, then he might agree.

I knock on the office door before stepping inside and closing it behind myself. "Luka," Mikhail says, glancing up from his computer. "What a night, huh?" He closes the laptop and cracks his knuckles.

I take a seat across from him in the black leather chair. "Yeah, I'll say." He's working late, so Madisyn is probably growing antsy waiting for him upstairs. "I was hoping I could talk to you about the situation with Hannah."

"That guy is a grade-A asshole. I'm glad you're looking out for her. It doesn't hurt that she's cute. Am I right?"

"You don't remember her?" I'm not sure why I thought that he might. He was with me that night at the bar, but he hadn't spoken with her and definitely didn't sleep with her.

"Am I supposed to?" Mikhail asks, a frown forming at the corners of his lips.

"Probably not. I hooked up with her a couple of years ago. Turns out the little girl, Bay, she's mine."

"Shit," Mikhail mutters under his breath. "Why didn't she try to track you down?"

"Hannah thought I worked at the club. I did wander behind the bar to grab us drinks that night, so I can see where she might have come to that assumption. She lost my number or something and didn't know how to reach me."

"You're a dad, huh?" Mikhail smirks. "Didn't see you beating me to the finish line."

"I didn't realize it was a competition." While Madisyn is pregnant, he's right. Me becoming a father overnight is quite a surprise.

"When isn't it a competition?" Mikhail chuckles. "What'd you want to talk to me about?"

At least Mikhail seems to be in a pleasant mood. "I don't like the thought of Hannah returning to her apartment."

Mikhail's gaze tightens. "You want Hannah to stay here under my roof?"

"That is what I'd like, indefinitely. With Bay being my daughter, it would be nice to have the opportunity to get to know her."

Mikhail pinches the bridge of his nose. "Hannah doesn't know what we do for a living. Do you see how this might be a problem?"

That thought has already crossed my mind. "She won't find out, sir. Madisyn will not tell her, and I'll make sure that we keep our business dealings away from her."

"She'll be living under our roof," Mikhail says. "She's bound to witness something that she shouldn't. Are you sure that she's loyal and won't run to the feds?"

"If she had any inkling of our business dealings, she wouldn't agree to stay."

"Can't say that I'm surprised. I suggest you make sure that she never finds out. Find out what she needs from her apartment and arrange to have the rest of her items brought to the compound or put into storage."

"Yes, sir," I say and stand.

"One more thing, Luka. If she's living here, I don't want any drama. You both need to discuss ground rules before committing to this idea of living together."

"Ground rules?"

What the hell is he talking about?

"Are you co-parents? Fuck buddies? If she wants to bring another man home, how will you deal with that situation?"

My hands ball into fists. "She's not bringing anyone home."

"Good," Mikhail says with a hint of a smirk. "Oh, and I'm going to have Nikita run background on Mark."

"Why? He's out of Hannah's life," I say. What's the point of digging up dirt on a man who may as well be dead to her?

Mikhail's jaw tightens. "Consider it a hunch. You might want to be rid of him, but I don't think he's smart enough to walk away."

Mikhail had better be wrong. "I'll look into it," I say.

"No." Mikhail holds up a hand. "You're too close to Hannah. It's better if it comes from another one of my men. If nothing turns up, Hannah never has to know."

"And if something does?"

"Nikita can be the bearer of bad news," Mikhail says.

———

Hannah is nowhere to be found. However, I suspect that she's locked away in her bedroom with Bay. I don't want to interrupt or bother her, especially if Bay's asleep.

Waking the little girl isn't going to win me any brownie points.

I'm not tired.

Pent-up energy flows through my veins. I spend an hour and a half in the gym pounding the shit out of one of the punching bags.

I should be exhausted.

My body is numb, from my knuckles that I've bruised to my heart. I shouldn't feel this way, constantly thinking about Hannah and Bay.

It doesn't help that I've welcomed her to live under my roof, technically Mikhail's. And I will owe him for his generosity.

Sweat coats my skin, and I grab a towel, shucking it over my neck. I'm hot and icy cold at the same time.

Each gasp is loud and raspy as I work to catch my breath from the workout. Keeping in shape is a requirement. I'm a bodyguard for the bratva, and I'd lay down my life for the men I vow to protect.

I run the towel through my hair and toss it in the laundry on my way out of the home gym. I knock full force into Hannah as she rounds the hallway's corner. Shouldn't she be in bed?

My hands reach up to her arms to steady her.

"Sorry," she apologizes. Hannah's gaze moves over my body from head to toe.

"What are you doing out of bed?" I ask as my hands remain on her forearms. My grip is firm but not harsh as the pads of my thumbs caress her bare skin.

She's in her pajamas. They're casual and comfortable, not the least bit sexy, but she still makes it look hot—dark blue plaid flannel bottoms and a solid navy t-shirt sink down past her hips. The evidence of Mark's abuse covers her collarbone and neck. I swear I can see bruising with a handprint around her throat.

Heat comes over me like a tidal wave. "He did this to you?" I already know the answer, but I still ask the question, appalled that any man would touch Hannah in such a manner.

He used his power to scare her. Terrorize her. And make her fear him.

What kind of animal must hurt a woman to force her to stay?

Hannah's soft voice breaks my concentration as I stare at the marks burned to her skin.

"It looks worse than it is," Hannah says.

"Don't justify his actions."

Hannah shrugs out of my grasp and covers the damage by brushing her hair forward with her fingers.

"I'm not," she says.

Hiding the scars doesn't make it go away. Doesn't she realize that? Hannah shuffles from one foot to the other, uncomfortable under my scrutiny.

"Can't sleep?" I ask. I am wondering why she's out of bed. It's nearly midnight.

"Yeah, I'm not great about sleeping in a new place."

It probably also had to do with what she's been through. Unwinding might help. I'd suggest a massage and an earth-shattering orgasm to put her to sleep if she was mine.

Instead, I opt for the second-best solution.

Alcohol.

"Come with me," I say and gesture for her to follow. I lead her to my office and close the door behind her. "Have a seat."

She laughs under her breath. "I feel like I've been sent to the principal's office," she jokes. She sits across from my desk and relaxes into the leather chair.

"Does that happen a lot with Bay?" The kid doesn't strike me as trouble, but I haven't been around Bay that much, a few hours last night, and I barely spent any time with her today.

A faint smile tugs at the corners of Hannah's lips. "No."

On the black filing cabinet behind my desk, is a silver platter with a bottle of scotch and two glasses. "Do you drink scotch?" I flip the glasses over and open the new amber bottle.

"Not usually," Hannah says. Her nose scrunches at my question.

"Sit tight," I say and hurry into the kitchen. The compound is quiet at this hour. Guards are working their shifts, but most are asleep or unwinding before bed.

I grab a few ingredients from the fridge and pantry and return with lemon juice, simple syrup, and club soda.

"What's that?" Hannah asks. She hasn't moved from the chair. Her hands clasped together in her lap.

"I'm making you a Scotch Collins."

"Oh," she says, and her head tilts slightly as she studies my movements.

I carry the ingredients to the table and prepare her bubbly drink. Her heated stare is on me the entire time. Even with my back to her, I can feel her watching me, studying what I'm doing.

It's good to be noticed.

To have won her attention, even if it's just while in my office.

"Here you go," I say and hand her the cocktail. I pour myself a scotch and perch myself at the edge of the desk.

Our knees brush against each other.

She blushes and sits up straighter, sipping her drink. "This is good," she says. "Although I'm not sure how it will help me get to sleep."

"You seem tense. I thought it might help you get out of your head."

"Is it that obvious?" Hannah offers a weak smile, and her attention is on her drink, her gaze downcast at the glass.

"You've been through a lot. Coming here to stay, I'm sure that can't be easy."

She tugs her bottom lip between her teeth. "It was only supposed to be for one night," she says, hardly above a whisper. Hannah glances up from her glass. "I don't want to be an imposition."

"You're not," I say and put my scotch glass on the desk. Leaning forward, I cup her chin, forcing her to look into my heated stare.

"You deserve so much better than that asshole." I'm still seething at what he did to her, the bruises visible under the fluorescent overhead lights.

She quirks a sly grin and sips the last of her liquor. "Yeah, that asshole couldn't even bring me to orgasm."

"Do you want another drink?"

"Yeah, I need it," she says and pushes the empty glass into my hands.

I stand and head across the room to mix her another drink. Already, she's grinning, and her cheeks are blushing. "You don't drink much, do you?" She seems tipsy.

"Kind of hard to get out. Being a full-time single parent puts a dent in my nightlife."

"What about your dating life?" I glance at her over my shoulder as I mix her second cocktail. I top off my scotch and hand her glass to her before resuming my position at the edge of the desk.

"Hasn't been anyone other than—" Hannah doesn't finish her sentence, and she shifts around in her seat, trying to get comfortable. Maybe it's the thought of *him* that's making her restless.

"You need a nickname for that asshole," I say.

"Other than asshat?" Hannah smirks. "What about orgasm killer?" She pins me with her stare, and I try not to choke on her remark.

"Orgasm killer?" I bring my scotch to my lips and take a swig. I need a stiff drink listening to her use the word *orgasm* and not getting aroused. She's gorgeous in her dark plaid pajama pants that are too big. Her cheeks are rosy, and I imagine that blush spreads down her neck across her breasts.

"That's all he was good for, killing any shot of me getting off. Do you know he could be called the two-minute man?"

My eyes widen, and I swallow the rest of the scotch as she rambles on about how awful Mark was in bed.

"Two minutes, that would actually be a record for him. There was no foreplay. Just wham, bam, and make sure you get it in the right hole! And don't get me started on him trying to talk dirty. Dirty talk should just be outlawed!"

"That's a bit harsh," I say.

She raises an eyebrow. I think I may have started a war with my *Zaya*. "Guys can't talk dirty. They think they can, but it comes out lame and not the least bit sexy."

I should leave it alone. Hannah's not thinking straight, but I disagree with her, and I'm not a man to sit idly by and accept what she's saying as the truth.

"Maybe two-minute man shouldn't be allowed to talk dirty, but I'm confident my filthy mouth would make you wet, and you'd be begging me to satisfy you." I pin her with my stare.

Hannah's lips part, and she gasps at my remark. Her cheeks burn, and she presses the glass to her lips, finishing her liquor. She hands me the empty glass. "Another?"

"I think you've had your limit," I say.

I can't imagine she'll be thrilled tomorrow when she remembers divulging all about how bad Mark was in bed.

She scrunches her nose in the most adorable way possible, and her bottom lip juts out as she pouts. "Pretty please? Or else I have to go to bed."

A dozen other ideas come to mind, and none of them involve sleep. "I'm not letting you get drunk."

Hannah giggles. "It's too late for that."

Two drinks.

That's all I gave her, and maybe they were a bit heavy on the scotch. I didn't precisely measure the liquor, but shit – she's toasted.

Hannah stands, ignoring my words, and saunters across my office toward the liquor.

"What do you think you're doing?" I raise a curious eyebrow. I've never known a woman to help herself to my alcohol or, really, anything in my home. Although, if I'm to be honest, Hannah is the first woman I've brought to the compound. Usually, my intimate activities are handled elsewhere.

"Getting myself a drink, silly!"

I'm glad she's feeling better, carefree, and happy. But I hate that the cause of that is the cocktails. I'd rather be the one helping her move on and get over that loser.

I push myself off the desk, placing my half-consumed glass of scotch on the wooden table as I close the distance between us. "No way."

"I'm tired of men telling me what I can and can't do. I'm an adult." Hannah stomps her bare foot as if she were trying to prove a point.

"Having a temper tantrum isn't a very grown-up thing to do," I whisper, coming up from behind. My hands are on either side of her, but I'm not touching her.

I want to touch her. I want to back her up against the desk, push down her pants and drop to my knees. I'd show her what it's like to have a riveting orgasm with her legs wrapped around my neck.

Has she forgotten what it was like when we were together? It was only one night, but I've never forgotten Hannah.

How could I?

I've slept with my fair share of women, but none of them came close. She's pure, innocent, and has no idea what I do for a living. That kind of secret makes the attraction hotter and much more deadly.

Hannah wiggles her butt into my groin. At least when I was wearing a suit, my clothes did a better job of hiding my desire.

But I'm in sweats and a t-shirt from working out in the gym. I didn't expect to stumble into Hannah late at night in the hallway.

She drags her hand into my hair, pulling me closer as she wriggles against me. "I want you to fuck me."

"I want that too," I whisper into her ear.

"Good," she says and spins around in my embrace. Her mouth is latched onto mine, and her arms wrap around my neck.

There's a sofa against the wall in my office, and I lift her into my arms and set her down on the black leather couch.

I straddle her frame, climbing atop her, pinning her arms above her head.

I should send her upstairs and tuck her into bed. But I'm no gentleman.

She whimpers and moans, wrapping her legs around me, her back arching and hips thrusting against mine. I can feel her desperation. But I'm not going to give her what she wants, not that quickly.

"I want to hear you scream my name," I whisper into her ear, not caring if it wakes the entire compound.

THIRTEEN

Hannah

I may have had two drinks, but I'm fully cognizant of what I'm about to do with Luka Ivanov in his office.

In the past two days, Luka has made me feel far more than that loser ever did. Why was I going to marry Mark?

Oh, right, stability.

Luka's hands are rough and strong as he pins me against the cold leather. His whispered words, "I want to hear you scream my name," cause me to shudder.

It's been too long since I've felt the impending tide wash over me. Sex had become a chore, a duty.

I get the feeling it won't be like that with Luka. It certainly wasn't the last time. How could I forget that night?

He drags his tongue along my neck, gasping as I struggle beneath his weight. I wrap my legs around him, pulling him down against me, wanting to feel his weight above.

"You want to come, don't you, *Zaya*?" His lips trail down to my stomach as he releases his hold on my arms.

"*Zaya*?" Is that his nickname for me?

I loosen my legs around him, letting him take control, just this once.

He doesn't answer in words. Luka inches my cotton shirt higher as his tongue dips into my navel, and he traces a path of warm kisses across my abdomen. His fingers tease the waistband of my bottoms, caressing my bare skin.

My stomach flutters from his touch.

"Condom?" I ask.

"Not something I keep in my office," Luka mumbles against my stomach.

"That's not why you keep a leather couch in your office?" I should feel relieved that he doesn't make it a habit of bringing women in here.

He smiles warmly, his eyes shining down at me. "No, it's not."

I move to sit up on the sofa, and Luka drags me back down.

He straddles my hips, his hands clenching mine, pinning them into the sofa. "Where do you think you're going?"

"You don't have a condom," I say.

"Not in my office. I have one upstairs, in my bedroom." He leans down, his lips teasing mine apart as I drink him in.

I want to kiss him. Taste him. Devour him.

"I didn't tell you my deepest, darkest secrets so that you'd have sex with me," I confess. That wasn't why I told him about Mark. I'm not sure why I said to him that the sex was terrible, and I've been craving the touch of a real man.

Luka's eyes glint. He doesn't move from his position above me, trapping me between him and the leather couch.

"Trust me, that's not why I'm doing this, *Zaya,*" Luka says. "You deserve to be worshipped, but I'm not a selfless man."

I lean up for a kiss, silencing him. He's set my body on fire, and I don't want this moment to end. Luka is nothing short of perfection, and I haven't even unwrapped the prize.

His lips move to my neck, and his hand grazes my side. I whimper from the recent bruises that Mark left on my skin. The scars are still fresh and sore.

Luka senses my discomfort. All sense of calmness is abandoned. "I'll kill him," Luka growls as his top lip snarls.

His words send a shiver down my spine. "This was a mistake," I say.

Luka's brow tightens. His scrutiny makes me feel as exposed as the wounds Mark left behind. I press a hand to Luka's chest and gently push him away.

I'm not ready for this, for us.

Luka moves off the sofa and gives me plenty of space. He runs his fingers through his hair, breathing deep and heavy as he steps farther back toward his desk.

"Are you mad?" I move to sit up on the sofa and fix my clothes that are a bit disheveled from our activities.

"Why would I be mad?" Luka asks. He drops his hands to his sides.

I don't answer. Isn't it obvious? "I disappoint you," I say.

He drops down to his knees, brushes a strand of hair behind my ear, and tilts my chin up to meet his stare. "You could never disappoint me, *Zaya.*"

"What about Hannah? Does Hannah disappoint you?" I ask. It sounds weird, my name coming out from my lips, but I don't know why he keeps calling me *Zaya.* That's not my name. Does he wish that I were someone else?

He pulls me onto his lap as he sits back down on the sofa. "It's a pet name, an endearment," Luka whispers. His fingers stroke my hair, playing with the strands. "You're mine." Luka's grip tightens as he holds me against him.

My mouth is dry, and my voice comes out hoarse and raspy. "Yours?" He's lost his mind. "We've known each other all of two days, Luka."

"We have a daughter together."

He's crazy. That's the only explanation for his possessiveness. "Yes, you helped conceive Bay, but she's my daughter."

"She's as much mine as she is yours." Luka's voice booms in the small space. "I'd have been there for her and you if I knew she existed."

I climb off his lap and stand, folding my arms across my chest. "I tried to get ahold of you. I did everything I could, I went back to the bar where we met, but no one knew who you were."

Doesn't he believe me?

"I know, you told me last night," Luka says. "I do not doubt you. I don't like that I missed out on Bay's birth, her first words, or first steps. I want to be there for her and you."

"You barely know me," I say. "It's crazy, me living here with you." Doesn't he think it's too soon? Why did I jump at the opportunity? I could get a hotel for a few nights and keep away from Mark just as easily.

Luka doesn't stand. He gives me space as he stares up at me. He clasps his hands together. His tone is firm and unapologetic but not the least bit threatening. "I disagree. Mark is out there, and until I know with absolute certainty that he won't hurt you or our daughter, I can't in good conscience let you leave."

I laugh at his words. He's not serious. "You're keeping me here against my will?"

He presses his lips together. "Don't turn this into a battle, Hannah. You're free to come and go as you please, but I don't trust Mark, and I don't think it's safe for you to return home."

"Mark's leaving my apartment." Isn't that what Luka told me? Mark understood it was over between us, and he would be out of our lives. "He's packing up his belongings, and he'll be gone soon."

"Yeah, but what will keep him from coming back? Men like Mark don't just go away on their own."

"What do you suggest I do?"

"I've already invited you to stay here," Luka says. He stretches his arms, putting them behind his head. "Why are we fighting?"

"I don't know. You started it," I blurt.

Luka stands and grabs me by the waist, putting me over his shoulder.

"Put me down!" I squeal.

"Do you trust me?" His voice is rough and deep.

It sends my stomach swooning. There's a dominance to him, something that Mark never possessed. He may have wanted to be dominant, but he was farthest from taking command.

"I barely know you," I whisper. My voice cracks, and he keeps me over his shoulder as he heads toward the office door.

"Can you keep quiet?"

No, I really can't.

I don't make an empty promise, and he exhales a heavy sigh and puts my feet down on the floor. "You really don't trust me. I ought to kill that douche bag who hurt you."

How do I answer that? He's not wrong, Mark is an asshole, but he wasn't always that way. Certainly not with Bay or me.

But there were signs, apparent red flags that I blatantly ignored. The first was how he treated his coworkers. He belittled them and bragged to me about his accomplishments.

"Come with me," Luka says, and he takes my hand, leading me out of his office.

I oblige. I follow Luka up the staircase. Is he taking me to my bedroom?

We wander past the door to my room, where Bay is sound asleep, and down toward the end of the hallway. His hand doesn't loosen its grip as he escorts me to the third floor.

"Where are you taking me?" I whisper, not wanting to wake anyone.

"You need to unwind, and I need another drink," Luka says.

Isn't that what got us into this mess in the first place? Well, at least tonight. "Are you sure that's a good idea?"

He drops hold of my hand and glances back at me over his shoulder. I suppose he's letting me go. If I want to leave and return to my room, I can. But I hate to admit I'm curious as to what he has in mind. I feel like the sex ship has already sailed.

He continues up the last few stairs, and I follow.

The corridor is dimly lit, the lights in the hall off except for a few scone lamps illuminating the path. There are several rooms, the doors closed for each one. Is this where the guards sleep?

We walk past three doors, and the fourth on the left, Luka opens the handle and steps inside. I follow behind him, and he flips on a lamp, casting the room in a soft, warm glow before closing the door.

"Are you tired?" Luka asks, glancing at me over his shoulder.

"Not really," I say. "I know it's late, but I think my brain is overstimulated." I'm going to pay for it tomorrow when I have to get up and Bay is wide awake at dawn.

"I hope you won't fight me on my next suggestion," he says and heads across the bedroom, opening a door.

Is that a closet? I stand, my feet firmly planted on the rug. "I swear, Luka if you're opening the door to a red room, I'm out of here."

He opens the adjoining door, flips on the light, and grins. "It's a bathroom," he says. "I'm surprised you know what a red room is, *Zaya*. I never took you for the type."

"I'm not," I say and clear my throat. Did it get warm in here?

"Right," he says with a smug smile. "I'll keep that in mind. You're not into a little rough play."

"Little rough play?" My jaw drops, and the grin only seems to grow on his face.

"Relax, *Zaya*. I'm going to draw you a bath. Just don't pass out. Okay? I'm not doing this for you to drown in the tub."

My shoulders relax. "Bath?" That's the only word that seems to have registered. "I could take a bath downstairs."

"You don't have your own jetted bathtub." Luka heads into the bathroom and turns on the faucet.

I tug my bottom lip between my teeth and fold my arms across my chest. The idea sounds fantastic but I'm not sure I should take a bath in Luka's room. "Are you trying to see me naked?"

"Maybe," Luka says with a wry grin. "But you can lock the door for privacy. And I'm a gentleman. I'll only burst in if there's a fire or if Bay's up," he says.

"Good to know where your priorities lie," I say, stepping closer and peeking into the bathroom.

It's not just any ordinary bathroom like I expect. It's the length of Luka's bedroom. While it's quite a bit narrower than his room, it's more luxurious than anything I'm used to seeing.

"This is all yours?" I gasp. "It's enormous!"

"Thank you," Luka says with a wry grin. "That is what every hot-blooded male loves to hear."

"Your bathroom. Get your mind out of the gutter." I nudge him with my shoulder as I step onto the warm tiles. "Oh my gosh! Even the floor is heated."

Luka shrugs and folds his arms across his chest. "It doesn't get used as often as it should."

"Do all of Mikhail's men have such luxurious accommodations? Maybe I should quit my day job and come work for your boss."

"Don't even think about it," Luka says, pinning me with his gaze.

His heated stare makes my mouth dry, and I swallow nervously. My voice comes out raspy. "Why not?"

Is he worried that we'll spend too much time with each other?

"It's late, and that is not a conversation we're having tonight," he mutters under his breath.

Luka grabs a folded towel from the closet and places it by the sink. "Do you need anything else?" he asks.

"I can't think of what. Thank you."

"My pleasure." Luka backs out of the bathroom, leaving me with the nearly ready bathtub.

He shuts the door, and I lock it behind him before undressing. I sink into the bath water and shut off the tap before turning on the jets.

It feels wonderful.

Do I need to worry about waking up the entire house from the noise of the bathtub jets?

Luka doesn't seem to worry. Why should I?

Every muscle in my body relaxes, and my racing mind finally can settle down. I've been in fight or flight mode since before leaving the apartment.

I close my eyes and am unsure how much time has passed.

The water is still warm but not scalding, but the tension in my shoulders seems to have melted away.

Luka bursts through the bathroom door.

I open my mouth to scream at him to get out when I realize that Bay is in his arms. Her face is red and splotchy.

"Bad dream," she sniffles and climbs out of Luka's arms.

After setting her feet down on the floor, he grabs the towel from the bathroom counter. "Sorry about interrupting you."

He's more gentlemanly than I thought, minus invading the bathroom with Bay. I thought I had locked the door, but he must have used a key to unlock it.

"I was done," I say. I'd spent long enough soaking in the water.

Grabbing the towel from his hands, I gesture for him to turn around.

I wrap the fluffy white towel around myself and unplug the tub.

Luka doesn't leave the bathroom. Although the space isn't crowded, his presence makes it feel smaller.

"Do you mind giving me some privacy?" I ask. I'm not quite ready for him to see me naked.

"Sure, I'll be just on the other side of that door." Luka heads out of the bathroom and quietly closes the door behind himself.

"Mama," Bay whines, and I bend down, hugging her and giving her a kiss. I'm trying not to get her pajamas wet, but she doesn't care.

I dry off as quickly as possible and toss my clothes on from earlier before lifting Bay into my arms as we head out of the bathroom.

Luka is seated at the edge of the bed. "I didn't know what to do with her."

"How'd you know she had a nightmare?" Bay was asleep on the second floor. I swear if he went downstairs and woke her so that he could steal a peek at me in the bath, I'll kill him.

"She climbed out of bed and started crying out in the hallway. One of the guards, Nikita, found her, and when he couldn't locate you, he came knocking on my door."

Bay rests her head on my shoulder and buries her hands against my chest as she snuggles up against me. I'm doing my best to keep my voice calm. I don't want to startle Bay. She's finally settling down and hopefully about to fall back to sleep.

"Why would he do that?" I ask.

"He knows about my relationship to you and Bay," Luka says.

There's no reason to hide it, but I'm surprised that word travels fast among Luka's colleagues. "Does everyone know?" I ask.

Luka shrugs. "Does it matter?"

He's right, it shouldn't, and soon enough those who don't know will find out. "It's late. We should be going to bed." I rub Bay's back, and she wiggles against me. Her breathing deepens, and I hope she'll fall asleep quickly once we get back to bed.

"Would you like me to walk you back to your room?"

"I think we can find it," I say. I head for the bedroom door, and Luka opens it for me.

"Let me carry Bay down the stairs."

As tempting an offer as that is, I doubt Bay will agree, and she's finally quiet. "I don't want to upset her. We'll be fine. Thank you, Luka."

I stroll out of his room with Bay in my arms and carefully navigate the stairs back to our bedroom. I tuck Bay under the covers. She instantly rolls onto her stomach, and her eyes shut as she drifts back to sleep.

It takes me longer to fall asleep, but it's late, and in a few hours, I'll have to be up and awake for Bay.

————

Dawn breaks before I'm ready to face the day. Bay has other ideas, bouncing on the bed, attempting to tickle me and making sure that I'm awake with her.

"Come on, let's get you ready for preschool."

After I shower and dress, I help Bay get out of her pajamas and put her in a romper. Brushing her hair, I style it into pigtails to keep it from getting tangled.

We hurry downstairs when we're finished getting ready, and I lift her onto the stool to sit at the counter for breakfast.

"Looking for something?" Luka asks.

I didn't hear Luka come into the kitchen. I glance back at him. He's already dressed in a classy black suit and tie with a crisp white shirt underneath.

"Cereal. Yogurt. Oatmeal. Something to feed Bay," I say, hoping that he'll have at least one of those items in the fridge or pantry.

"There's pancake batter. Eggs and bacon are also in the fridge."

Bay scrunches her nose and sticks out her tongue. None of those sound desirable to my kid. She's incredibly picky, and it doesn't matter how many different foods I encourage her to try; she always sticks to the same things.

"We can swing by the store this morning on the way to your apartment and pick up something she'll eat," Luka says.

"I need to drop her off at preschool before going to the apartment."

Luka steps farther into the kitchen, past the island and counter. He opens the fridge and grabs a bottle of orange juice. "Do you like this stuff?" he asks, shaking the bottle and eyeing Bay.

She nods vigorously, a huge grin spreading across her face.

"She doesn't get juice that often," I say.

"What mother doesn't give her kid orange juice?" Luka asks.

I fold my arms across my chest. "Are you questioning my parenting choices?" He's known he's a father for a weekend, and already, he thinks he knows what's best for my daughter.

With the orange juice bottle in one hand, Luka holds his arms up in surrender. "I didn't intend for this to be a fight."

I fumble through the cabinets, searching for drinkware. After opening the fourth cabinet, I reach for the smaller-sized juice glass and place it on the counter.

"Is this for you or Bay?" Luka asks.

"Bay," I say.

He fills the glass halfway before sliding the orange juice across the counter.

"Can I borrow your phone before we head to the apartment?" I ask.

"Depends on who you plan on calling."

Does he think that I'd reach out to Mark? I didn't get enough sleep last night. I'm doing my best not to pick an argument with Luka, but everything seems to piss me off this morning.

"My boss at work. I missed yesterday's shift, and I'd like to explain to her what's going on. I would have gone in this morning to speak with her, but I should probably grab a few things from the apartment."

"What do you need from your place? I'll pick it up for you," Luka says.

"That isn't necessary. I can swing by after I drop Bay off at preschool."

Luka retrieves his cell phone from his pocket and unlocks the device before handing it to me. "I'll watch Bay while you talk to your boss."

"Thank you," I say, taking the phone from his grasp. I head out of the kitchen and dial the phone number for work. I press the phone to my ear, and just as I reach the hallway, Bay's voice carries across the room.

"Are you my daddy?" Bay asks.

I glance over my shoulder as Bay stares up at Luka and hear a rough "Hello?" on the opposite end of the phone.

FOURTEEN

Luka

Bay just asked me if I'm her father.

Hannah has impeccable timing. She's on the phone with her boss, or pretending to be, the moment that she hears Bay's voice.

"Yes," I say. I don't intend to lie to Bay. It wasn't my choice not to be involved in her life from the beginning.

She brings the glass of juice to her lips with two hands and finishes the drink. "More juice?"

"Does your mom let you have more juice?" I ask.

Bay's lips close, but her smile grows wider as she tilts her chin up at me. I'm guessing that's a no. "Please?"

I refill Bay's glass halfway with orange juice. It beats having to talk about being her biological father with her. That's a conversation for Hannah to partake in when the time is right.

Bay brings the glass to her lips with two hands and sips at her orange juice.

Hannah breezes back into the kitchen and hands me back my cell phone.

"Is everything okay with work?"

"Yeah, I have to go in later this afternoon to cover a shift. Any chance I can have you swing by the preschool and pick Bay up?" Hannah tugs her bottom lip between her teeth.

Is she nervous, asking me to look after Bay?

"I think I can handle that," I say. "Assuming the school lets me take her home."

"When I drop her off this morning, I'll make sure to add you to the pickup list."

"And remove Mark from that list."

I don't want him showing up and kidnapping Bay. The man is already unhinged. Any opportunity that he has to get to Hannah and hurt her, I wouldn't put it past him.

Bay finishes her glass of orange juice, and then the three of us head to the car. There's an extra booster seat in the garage from Mikhail's sister's kids, the twins, who lived at the compound.

I grab the booster and secure it into the backseat before Bay climbs into the car.

"You just happen to have a spare booster seat?" Hannah's brow is tight, and she folds her arms across her chest.

"Like the toys I gave to Bay the other day to play with, the booster seat was for Mikhail's niece and nephew. There used to be twins running around the halls."

Hannah smiles weakly. "I can't imagine. Although the house does seem more child-proof than I would have thought." She climbs into the front seat passenger side once she's satisfied that Bay is buckled into the booster seat.

The car is a push button, and I start the engine, waiting for Hannah to buckle her seatbelt. "Do you want me to swing by the grocery store to pick up a few breakfast items now, or do we have time to grab a bite out to eat?" I don't know what time Bay is supposed to be at preschool.

"Just stop at the grocery store and I'll run in really quick," Hannah says.

I'm not thrilled about her going anywhere alone, but I doubt Mark will be there. I've already run my plans by Mikhail, taking the day to help Hannah. He was agreeable, especially after last night and Mark showing up at the compound.

I exit through the gates and head onto the main road, ensuring that we're not being followed.

"Are you sure he won't be at the house?" Hannah asks, glancing at me as I head toward the grocery store.

She fidgets with her hands. I can sense she's anxious, and while she's trying to portray that she's calm and collected for Bay, I see right through the charade.

"If he is, he won't stick around." I have a spare gun in the glovebox. I'm not packing heat on me. The last thing I want is for Hannah to ask questions and grow fearful of what I do for a living.

Besides, I don't plan on leaving Hannah alone until I drop her off at work, and even without a weapon, I can take out Mark's ass single-handedly.

"I hope you're right," Hannah whispers. She glances out the side window and emits a soft sigh.

"Do you want to stay in the car while I run into the grocery store?"

She smiles weakly and shakes her head. "That isn't necessary. I'll be quick. In and out in just a few minutes."

I'd have asked one of Mikhail's other guards to come with us if I was worried, but Hannah will be fine.

I keep glancing in the rearview. There's traffic but no vehicles following us. It also helps that I ditched the sim card for Hannah's phone because I'm sure that's how Mark tracked her down last night.

I pull up to the front of the store and unlock the vehicle. Hannah hurries out and straight inside through the automatic doors.

In under five minutes, she's back with two plastic bags of groceries. "All that for breakfast?" I ask as she climbs back into the car.

"Bay is going to need to bring a bagged lunch to preschool. And I'll have her eat breakfast when she gets there, too, rather than have her wear yogurt and get it all over your car."

I chuckle. "The car can be detailed. It's not a big deal. What time do I pick her up?"

Hannah grabs the seatbelt and yanks it across her chest, snapping the buckle into the latch. "Pick-up is at 2:30."

"I'll make sure I'm there early. Relax," I say and reach over, resting my hand on her arm. "I can handle looking after my daughter."

Hannah inhales a sharp breath.

"What?" I ask.

She glances back at Bay, who doesn't seem even slightly interested in our conversation. "What did you say when she asked if you were her—"

"Daddy?" I repeat Bay's earlier remark. "Yes. I wasn't going to lie to my daughter, but I also didn't get into an explanation about it."

"Okay, good." Hannah's shoulders relax.

I pull away from the grocery store, and Hannah gives me directions to the preschool. It's across town, in the opposite direction of the compound.

Traffic is heavy, and when we finally arrive, the three of us go inside together. I want to make sure they know who I am and recognize me later when it's time for me to pick Bay up this afternoon.

After Hannah fills out the paperwork and makes updates to it, including removing Mark from the list, we head outside.

I nudge her as we walk, brushing up against her. "I have to ask, is this place special?"

"What do you mean?" Hannah stops walking and turns to face me.

"The preschool is across town. The neighborhood is nice, but there are closer places that we could enroll Bay."

"You want to change preschools because it's inconvenient for you to drop her off?" Hannah shakes her head and knocks past me, heading for the car. "Don't worry. You won't have to drop her off or pick her up again after today."

"Hannah, that's not fair." Doesn't she realize that if they're going to be living with me at the compound, this place is a pain in the ass drive to get to? There are plenty of other preschools nearby. I can count four that we passed on the way.

She climbs into the front seat and slams the door shut.

I walk around the car and open the driver's side door. I start the engine but don't put the car in reverse to back out of the space yet. "Why are we fighting?"

"You want to change Bay's preschool. She's happy here. She has friends, and I doubt she will be excited about starting a new school."

"Is that what this is about? Because I'll drive across town and drop her off if that's what is best for my daughter."

Hannah folds her arms across her chest. She shifts in her seat. While she's silent, she always seems quite antsy. Like she's holding back.

"Tell me, *Zaya*, what is it?" I can't help her if I don't know what's going on.

"I can't afford any other preschools."

"You don't have to worry about finances regarding Bay. She's my daughter too, and I fully intend to help. Let me worry about paying for her education."

Hannah's jaw drops. "I'm not asking for a handout."

"Don't worry. I wasn't giving one." I'm tired of fighting with her. I focus my attention on the parking lot and put the car into reverse, backing out of the space.

She's silent for the rest of the drive, all fifteen minutes. It would have been less if traffic wasn't quite so heavy for a Monday.

I pull up out front of her building and parallel park the car in a space.

"You don't have to come in with me," Hannah says.

She may not want me to come in, but I'm not letting her go upstairs alone. Mark could be waiting for her.

Is that why she's moody?

Is she worried that she might come face-to-face with him?

"I know, but I want to make sure it's safe and he's not waiting upstairs for you." I accompany Hannah inside.

A heavy silence falls over us while we shuffle into the elevator.

It's not uncomfortable like the stifling car ride.

Once we reach the third floor, she pulls out her house keys, fiddling with them on the way upstairs.

As we approach her door, I keep my voice low. "Unlock it, but I want you to stay here while I make sure he's not anywhere inside."

Hannah's voice trembles as she speaks. "Don't be ridiculous." She's probably trying to convince herself that everything is fine.

And it will be if she follows my instruction.

She slides the key into the lock but steps aside to let me enter. I turn the handle and step into the apartment. The lights are off, and I leave it alone, not wanting to alert anyone to my presence.

I search every room, closet, and even behind the bath curtain. There's no sign of Mark or anyone else for that matter. However, there is a red envelope on the bed. In black cursive marker, the envelope reads *Hannah*.

I grab the envelope and shove the contents into my jacket pocket. If it's a threatening letter, I don't want to upset her by letting her read it. And if it's not and it's an apology, I doubt the bastard means it. He's probably just trying to swindle his way back into her heart.

Either way, the letter is bad news.

She never has to see it. Besides, I vowed to protect her from that loser.

"It's clear," I say, waiting for Hannah to come inside.

Hannah steps into the entryway of the apartment and flips on the light. "His stuff is still here," she says with a sigh.

I pull out my cell phone from my pocket. "Did you take any pictures in case he damages the place?" My cousin went through a nasty divorce, and I remember his lawyer warning him to document everything.

"I didn't even think about it," Hannah says.

She's quiet, reserved, and heads with precision through the hallway, past the living room, right for the bedroom.

"Do you want help?" I offer, not wanting to overstep. She grabs a duffel bag from under the bed and unzips it.

"Sure, grab some clothes of mine from the dresser."

She already had one suitcase at the compound, but she also hadn't planned on staying indefinitely with me when she packed. I'm honestly surprised she had time to pack, but I'm sure it wasn't like she neatly folded her clothes. She probably stuffed as much as she could and as quickly as possible.

I open the top drawer and try not to gawk at the lacy panties and bras. There's a lot to carry across the room, and it'd be easier just to remove the drawer from the dresser. I pull the drawer out of its track and bring the contents to the duffel bag, dumping all her sexy underwear inside.

Hannah stands by the closet, pulling her clothes off the hangers, one at a time. She glances over her shoulder at me and raises an eyebrow.

"Are you terrified to touch my panties?"

"No." I didn't think she'd want me to touch her undergarments. I reach my hand into her duffel bag and retrieve a black lacy thong with my fist. "Do I look like I have a problem touching your panties? I'll have you know, I'd rather touch the ones you're wearing than clean ones any day."

Her cheeks burn, and she glances back at the closet, avoiding eye contact with me. "You can put that back in the bag."

I release my grip and let her panties fall back into the duffel. "Sure. Whatever you want, *Zaya*." Before clearing out the next drawer, I bring the drawer back to the dresser and slide it on the track.

We've made several trips to my car in under an hour, loading it with clothes for both Hannah and Bay, along with several trash bags filled with Bay's toys. Had I known she was short on luggage, I'd have brought several bags and scrounged a few boxes.

"Anything else?" I ask. Her apartment is heavily furnished, but I can work with a few of our men to transport her belongings to the compound or storage. That can wait for another day. The goal is to get everything that she needs or may need for the foreseeable future.

Hannah heads into the living room toward the coffee table. She bends and opens the drawer, retrieving a photo album featuring a tiny handprint on the cover. It must be baby pictures of Bay.

"Yeah, now I'm ready."

On the way out of the apartment, Hannah grabs her car keys, and we head downstairs together. "I'm going to follow you to work. Just to make sure that Mark isn't there when you show up."

"Luka, that's a bit overkill. Don't you think? I'll be fine. The medical center has security, and he doesn't even know that I'm working this afternoon. It's not my usual shift."

"Fine, I'm heading to the coffee shop a block away from the medical center."

"There are plenty of other coffee shops closer." Hannah unlocks her car door and steps out into the street. She's parked a few cars away from me.

I wait until she's in her car before walking to mine. "Yeah, but they have the best biscotti," I say. I've never even tried biscotti, but fuck, I'm not letting her out of my sight until I know that she's safe.

If I knew where Mark was right now, I wouldn't be so concerned. And while he's supposed to be at work, I worry that he's unhinged and going to do something to Hannah.

FIFTEEN

Hannah

"He followed me to work," I say, explaining to Madisyn how my morning has gone.

She's covering a double shift, which sucks for her, but I'm grateful to have her company and someone to talk to when I have the time.

"He's protective," Madisyn says. "It's not necessarily a bad trait. He just wants to make sure that you're safe."

"And following me all the way to work—it's overkill." Doesn't she realize it has stalker vibes written all over it? "It's like a huge red flag."

"So, break up with him." Madisyn glances at me as she taps away at the computer at the nurse's station.

"We're not dating," I say. "How would that even work?" I grab my mug of coffee and take a sip. It's not nearly as good as the coffee from the café down the street, but there was no chance that I was stopping there while Luka followed me to work.

Grimacing, the coffee is bitter and scalding hot.

"You tell me, you're the one who had his kid," Madisyn says. "Listen, I get the situation is unique. You both need to figure out a balance, what you each want, and go from there."

"Is it bad that I want him?" I mutter into my cup.

Madisyn chuckles, apparently hearing my remark.

Shit.

"So, tell him that," Madisyn says. "He's a complicated guy, and there's a lot that you don't know about Luka, but give him a chance. Just recognize that he's protective. And it's not always a flaw for a character trait. The man would lay down his life for Bay and you."

"I'm not asking him to lay down his life for us," I say.

"Yes, but if you're getting involved with Luka, even as just co-parents, you need to realize the kind of man he is and what he'd do for his family."

She couldn't have told me about his overprotective nature before introducing us? Although in her defense, running into him at the bar wasn't part of the plan.

"Do you know that I still remember that night, when the two of us conceived Bay?"

"I'd hope you remember sleeping with him!" Madisyn giggles, not quite understanding.

"I still think about it. About him. It's probably because he's Bay's biological father, and I'm tied to him forever."

Madisyn shifts on the chair, folding her arms across her chest and giving me a pointed look. "Forever? Eighteen years, probably fifteen now."

Is that supposed to make me feel better about the situation?

"Luka's not like any other man whom you'd date. He's the complete opposite of Mark, who I never really cared for if I'm honest. You should give Luka a shot."

"You mean Luka's a good guy?" I take another swig of my coffee and grimace. "Needs more sugar."

She coughs and turns the chair back to her computer. "I've got a lot to get done today. Catch you later?"

"Yeah, of course." Is she brushing me off or busy with work?

I can't tell, but the fact she has to work a double shift makes me think it's not me.

———

I round the corner of the hallway, slamming head-first into Mark. "What are you doing here?" My stomach tenses, and I take a step back, skimming the hall searching for Madisyn or anyone else should the need arise.

I don't trust Mark, and while we're in a public building with plenty of security, he shouldn't be here.

"Did you get my letter? We need to talk," Mark says. He grasps my arm, his fingers digging in tight around my skin.

"Get off me." I grit my teeth and yank my arm free from his clutches. What the hell is he talking about? "What letter?"

"It's about your new boyfriend. The one you're playing house with," Mark says.

"I don't want to hear it." The nearest exit is behind him, which doesn't help me. I hustle in the opposite direction, through the long corridor, past several patient rooms. The last thing I want is to put one of their lives in jeopardy by seeking shelter there.

Mark's footfalls thud across the linoleum flooring as he chases after me, grabbing me by the shirt and spinning me around to face him.

"I've had enough with your games and antics, Hannah. You're coming with me."

I stomp my foot onto his toe and knee him in the groin. "I'm not going anywhere with you!"

It's enough to startle him, and he drops his grip on me.

Madisyn rushes out into the hallway from around the corner. "Get out of here!" she shouts at Mark. "I've already notified security. We'll press charges and have your ass arrested if you stick around."

Mark takes a step back, seeming to get the message. He holds his hands up in mock surrender. "I'll catch up with you later, Hannah."

"Don't!" I scowl and point at the door, fuming. "I never want to see you again." My hands ball into fists at my side. Adrenaline pumps through my veins as he retreats for the elevator, shoulders slumped.

He's pretending to be defeated. I can feel the deception across the hall. It's an act. Maybe Mark should have chosen a different profession. His fictitious persona is good. I believed that he was someone else all along. He had me fooled.

Madisyn chases after Mark, ensuring that he takes the elevator down. When she's satisfied that he's gone, she strides toward me. "Are you okay?" she asks, glancing me over. "Did he hurt you?"

I rub at my arm. "I'll be fine. Just a little sore from his grip."

"You should file a police report," Madisyn says as she lifts my sleeve higher. His fingers have left a thick red mark which will likely turn into a bruise.

"It's fine. What are they going to be able to do? I need to get back to work. I still have patients to check on."

"Hannah," Madisyn calls after me.

I ignore her. It's bad enough that I'll have to face her at home, and I'm sure she'll tell Luka, and if not, Mikhail certainly will when she confides in him what happened.

I trust Madisyn, but not to keep a secret about Mark.

———

I have a few more hours until my shift is over. Glancing at the clock on the wall, Luka should have picked up Bay from preschool by now. I haven't heard a peep from the school or Luka.

Madisyn strolls up to me, glancing at my arm. My sleeve does a decent job hiding the bruise that Mark left behind.

"I'm heading out."

"I thought you were working a double?" I ask.

Madisyn is already changed out of her work scrubs. She has her purse slung over her shoulder. "I was, but I got called to the principal's office," she says with a smirk.

"I never knew that was a good thing." The smile on her face is as genuine as I've seen, but I can't quite determine why she's always so damn cryptic with me. I've given up trying to make sense of her life and what she's up to. If she wants to confide in me, she will.

Madisyn rests a hand on her belly. "My doctor's appointment got moved up. Mikhail is going to drive me home after."

"Is everything okay?"

"It's fine. Are you sure you're okay here? Do you want me to have Mikhail send up one of his men to keep an eye on the floor?"

The smile disappears from my face. "Like a bodyguard?" That sounds dreadful and embarrassing. "I don't need a babysitter."

"It's not for you. It's to make sure that Mark doesn't come back," Madisyn says. She heads toward the elevator, and I walk with her down the hallway. I'm heading in that direction anyhow, to the nurse's station.

Should I be worried? "Does this look like the face of a girl who's concerned?"

Madisyn hits the button for the elevator. She glances over her shoulder back at me. "You're tough, I get that, but Mark isn't just going to walk away. I've dealt with men like him before."

"I'm staying with Luka. It'll be fine."

Her brow tightens, and a scowl crosses her face. "I'm just worried that's not enough. I'll talk to Mikhail—"

"Please, don't." I step behind the nurse's station. I want this conversation to be over. Can she get into the elevator already and leave?

"Fine, but you need to tell Luka that Mark stopped by tonight."

That's a conversation that I'm not looking forward to having with Luka. "I will, but let me finish work first."

The elevator doors open, and Madisyn steps inside. I'm relieved that she's gone. I realize that she's only trying to help, but it's getting on my nerves. Was moving in with them a bad idea?

Besides, how many grown men live with their boss? I still can't quite wrap my head around the situation other than Mikhail must be a very wealthy individual and always requires extensive security.

But even billionaires allow their employees to go home. Don't they?

SIXTEEN

Luka

Picking Bay up from preschool is easier than I imagined. I drive her back to the compound and bring her into the study with the box of toys.

I have one of the guards, Anton, help unload my car with Hannah's possessions. Most of it is brought up to her room, except for one of the bags of toys. I request that Anton bring that into the study for Bay.

The overhead light is harsh, and I dim the lights and sit on the sofa while keeping an eye on Bay.

I can't expect Mikhail or any other guards to babysit Bay, nor would I want them to. She is my daughter. I want to take the time to get to know her.

Bay plops down by the fireplace. The hearth is off, but she doesn't care much either way. Grabbing the fire engine and police cruiser from the box, she rolls them around on the floor.

An entire box of toys and the kid has latched onto two items.

They must be her favorite.

Or she likes toy cars.

It feels like forever since tiny feet were pitter-pattering through the compound. It wasn't that long ago that Aleksandra resided under Mikhail's roof with the twins, Sophia and Liam.

I was supposed to marry Aleksandra, protect her, move to Russia to keep her and the twins safe. It had all been under Mikhail's orders, and while we had been well acquainted with one another, I never desired Aleksandra.

I follow orders—specifically, Mikhail Barinov's.

Strolling down memory lane isn't for the weak.

My stomach tenses, remembering what I did to Aleksandra, the pain that I caused her. She betrayed the family and ended up marrying an Italian Don. It probably was to spite Mikhail, and it worked.

I hope she's happy now that she has the life she always wanted.

If I had married her, I'd have never known about my daughter, Bay. I'd have been in Russia commanding the bratva, giving orders to our men.

Strange how fate has a way of revealing itself. Marrying her would have hurt both of us, but I'd have done it for Mikhail.

I'm a prince of darkness, not a hero.

Hannah has no idea of the underworld or what we dabble in daily. She's kept blind from the laundering that happens under our roof to the assassins and smugglers. Our men, the soldiers who work for Mikhail, handle everything, from illegal papers to cleaning up the bodies of our enemies.

"Daddy," Bay's sweet voice jars my attention.

My mouth is dry at her simple word. "Yes, tiger?" I ask and lean forward, my hands clasped together on my lap.

She stands and approaches me on the couch. "Hungry. Snack time."

Hannah hadn't mentioned giving her a snack or feeding her. Although Bay will have to eat dinner, Hannah won't be back until near bedtime.

"What do you like to eat?" I ask.

Why do I feel that everything she will list off we don't have in the pantry or fridge?

"Chocolate pudding, chocolate cake, chocolate ice cream."

"I'm noticing a theme," I say and pull Bay into my lap. "Let me guess, your favorite food is chocolate?"

Bay nods enthusiastically. Her blue eyes shine brightly up at me.

"Does your mom let you eat all those things before dinner?"

The little tyke scrunches her nose and giggles. "Please?"

If she weren't my kid, I probably wouldn't give in so quickly, but damn, that smile and those wide baby blues. "Come on, let's see what we can find in the kitchen," I say.

I lift her from the sofa and carry her on my hip out of the study and into the kitchen.

"Daddy, chocolate."

Bay isn't the least bit shy about saying what she wants. I'll bet she gets that from her mother.

"And your mom won't get mad if you have chocolate before dinner?" I ask.

It's almost four in the afternoon, and soon we'll have to figure out what to eat for dinner. I'm not sure what the kid eats, but I'm sure she'll tell me what she doesn't eat.

It's not just the resemblance to Hannah that is uncanny. Everything from her expressions and mannerisms to the baby blue eyes and brunette hair. I swear Hannah could have been cloned.

But the longer I stare at Bay, I see pieces of me in her, specifically her determination. It's not that I'm a picky eater, but I do know what I want, and I don't let anyone stand in my way. I get the sense Bay will grow up and become a lot like me.

I'm not sure if that's good or bad if I'm to be honest with myself.

We scrounge through the kitchen, and I find a half dozen chocolate chip cookies in the pantry. I allow Bay to have one and hope that will suffice until dinner.

I have her seated at the edge of the counter as I stand in front of her to make sure that she doesn't fall.

"Milk," she says as she waves the cookie in my face.

"Don't move," I warn and turn my back to grab the gallon of milk from the fridge.

She doesn't budge. At least the kid is a good listener.

I pour her a glass of milk and bring it to the counter. She dunks the cookie into the milk before taking a bite, leaving crumbs everywhere.

"You're supposed to do that with Oreos," I say.

Her eyes light up, and her mouth opens. I can already sense her next question.

"We're fresh out of stock."

Bay's shoulders slump as she nibbles on her cookie, dunking it into the glass of milk before taking another bite.

"There you are!" Mikhail blazes into the kitchen with Madisyn right on his heel. Those two have been inseparable since she forced her way into the compound.

"What's going on?" I ask, glancing between them as Madisyn comes to stand beside Mikhail, her arms folded across her chest.

"Mark decided to show up this afternoon at work."

Heat rages through me. "What?" I grab Bay and place her feet onto the floor.

She reaches above her for the counter, wanting her glass of milk.

"Here," I say and hand her the glass as she finishes the last of her cookie.

"We kicked him out, but I'm concerned he might wait around for her to leave," Madisyn says.

"Can you watch Bay? I need to get to the hospital," I say. Her shift isn't over for several more hours, but she shouldn't be alone. If Mark shows up, there should be someone watching her back.

"Of course," Madisyn says as she brushes past me.

Bay drops her glass of milk, the contents spill, and glass shatters on the floor. The little one's eyes water, and her bottom lip pout. "Sorry." She sniffles and her hands tremble.

"It's okay. I'll clean this up," Madisyn says. She lifts Bay from the ground and places her on the counter.

"Are you sure?" I'm torn between helping with Bay and looking after Hannah. I can't be in two places at once.

"Yes. Go! It'll be good practice," Madisyn says. She shoos us out of the kitchen while cleaning up the pieces of broken glass on the floor.

"I'm coming with you," Mikhail says, glancing at his phone.

"What is it?" We head to the garage, and I grab the keys to the SUV. We have a dozen vehicles that we use whenever the need arises—everything from pickup trucks and SUVs to sports cars and sedans.

The keys to the midnight black SUV hang on the wall. I hit the button to open the garage and snag the keys before heading for the driver's side door.

"I had Anton put surveillance on Hannah's place after the two of you left this afternoon. Mark is there right now. How about we pay him a visit?" Mikhail suggests.

"Hopefully, Mark is packing his shit and getting the hell out of town," I mutter. I yank open the front door and climb onto the seat before starting the engine.

Mikhail yanks his seatbelt across his lap and snaps it in place. "Only one way to find out."

I put the SUV in drive and clench the steering wheel as I pull out of the garage and down the driveway for the metal gates.

The guard on duty opens the gate as he sees us approach. Mikhail gives a brief nod at the gentleman working the front entrance.

"How are we doing this?" I ask.

The street in front of the compound is residential, the area not too congested, but as we head farther into the city and closer to the apartment complex, it's clear that it's rush hour.

Mikhail grabs his phone and opens the app to check on Mark. "He's still there." Mikhail huffs under his breath.

"What?"

"Bastard isn't even packing. He's in the living room watching television."

I glance at Mikhail. "And how do you know that?"

"Camera's installed in both the hallway and living areas," Mikhail says as he lifts his phone, showing me the screen. There are a half dozen views with different angles and camera surveillance monitoring her apartment.

"It's good Hannah's not living there anymore," I say. She'd be livid if she found out Mikhail had surveillance equipment installed inside her apartment.

She doesn't have to find out.

Besides, she's not moving back to her apartment. There's no reason for her to live there, and I don't want Mark showing up uninvited, letting himself in like he owns the place and they're still together.

Traffic is heavy and inches along. I cut off another vehicle to change lanes and make a sharp right at the next intersection. I can't stand sitting in traffic, especially when I'm driving.

"You're welcome, by the way, for letting Hannah and your daughter live under my roof."

Is Mikhail looking for a thank you card?

"It's appreciated," I say, my voice gruff. I'm concentrating on getting us to the apartment and how I will handle Mark. I took the SUV, so putting him in the trunk isn't the best option.

We could rough his ass up, but he'll recognize us, and he knows where we live. I wouldn't care, but he seems like the type of guy who would run to the cops, begging for protection. We've had enough trouble with the feds, and we don't need them knocking on our door.

Mikhail may have managed to win one of them over and turn her, but he isn't likely to do that to the entire department.

"You really didn't know you were a father until this weekend?" Mikhail asks. He shifts in his seat, getting comfortable as he glances at me.

I'm not the least bit relaxed, and we're having this conversation, now?

"She didn't know how to reach me," I say. I've already told him the story. Is he second-guessing what happened? My loyalty lies with him.

Mikhail strokes his jaw and chuckles under his breath. "Then, it's a good thing you never married my sister. Shit. Imagine if you had, what a fuck show that would have been. You in Russia and Hannah here."

"Are you trying to say you're happy that Aleksandra married an Italian?" I never thought I'd see the day when the Russian Bratva and the Italian Mafia would co-exist. We're not friends, but we do keep to ourselves. We have an understanding.

"I wouldn't go that far," Mikhail says. His gaze tightens as he glances out the window avoiding my stare.

Traffic inches forward, and I make a left this time, jogging through narrow alleyways to get to the apartment.

There's an empty parking space out front, and I squeeze the SUV into the narrow spot. The moment the engine is off, we climb out of the vehicle and slam the door shut in unison.

We head inside and up to her unit. I don't have a key. I knock on the front door, and Mikhail covers the peephole to keep Mark from seeing us on the other side of the door.

Heavy footfalls fumble over the floor, and then he unlocks the door without so much as asking who is on the opposite side.

"I thought we told you to leave?" I grab Mark by the lapels and shove him backward, dragging his ass to the living room, pinning him against the wall. I shove my forearm up into his throat.

Mikhail shuts the door behind us, making sure the neighbors don't get a show.

We're not exactly on friendly terms with the cops.

"Do you like harassing women?" I'm ready to tear him apart, limb by limb.

"What? Of course not." Mark is scrawny and pale. He's like a string bean against the wall. It wouldn't take much to snap him in half.

"Do you have a weapon?" Mikhail asks as I keep Mark flush against the wall.

He's in sweatpants and a white t-shirt. I doubt that he's carrying anything dangerous.

"I'm not answering that!" Mark's top lip snarls, but I can see the fear in his eyes. He's trying to be tough, and it doesn't matter to me whether it's because there are two of us or he's intimidated.

"Search him," I say, glancing at Mikhail.

I keep Mark positioned against the wall, and Mikhail pats him down, satisfied that he's not harboring a gun or pocketknife. "He's clean."

"I wouldn't go that far," I seethe and yank him from the wall, forcing him down onto his knees.

I whip out my gun and unlock the safety, pointing it at Mark's head.

"You don't have a silencer on that gun," Mark says. "You'll never get away with this. I'll tell Hannah!"

"You're just giving me more reasons to shoot you," I say.

But he is right. There isn't a silencer, and neighbors are bound to hear the gunshot and glance out into the hallway or out their window.

I don't like witnesses.

"For every problem, there's a solution." Mikhail pulls out his gun and attaches a silencer tucked inside his coat pocket.

"Please, I swear I'll leave Hannah alone," Mark begs. He's not much of a fighter. It rather takes the high out of the kill.

"We've already warned you once," I say. "You were instructed to stay away, pack up your shit, and leave."

"I was packing," Mark says.

"Where are the boxes?" Mikhail asks. He takes his gun with the silencer attached, poking through the apartment. "I don't see any boxes. Do you see any boxes, Luka?"

"All I see is a liar," I say, staring down at Mark.

Mark knocks my leg with his arm, using his weight to trip me up. The nitwit decides to fight back.

He scrambles across the floor and attempts to stand, reaching for the door handle.

I tackle Mark to the ground, smashing his face into the wood floor, breaking his nose. The crunch of bones isn't pleasant, and blood pours down his face.

Mark wipes at the blood as it drips, leaving a disaster that will require the clean-up crew before Hannah steps foot in this place again.

Mikhail stands watching the ordeal, the gun still poised in his right hand. "Are we going to finish him or let him crawl home to his mommy for dinner?"

I'd like to finish his ass, put a bullet in his head, and never worry about him bothering Hannah or my daughter. "Give me the gun," I say, holding out my hand to Mikhail.

"You're too close to Hannah," Mikhail says. "When she asks, and inevitably, she will, you can't have your hands dirty with his blood."

"Yes! Yes! You should let me live," Mark says, his eyes widening with excitement. He rises to his knees and pushes himself up to stand.

"Get your ass back on the ground," I shout at Mark, knocking him back down to the floor. "I warned you yesterday that if you harassed Hannah, I'd kill you. Showing up at her work today constitutes bothering her. Did you think it was an empty threat?"

I swore to Hannah that I'd protect her.

This falls on me.

Hannah is my responsibility.

SEVENTEEN

Hannah

I change out of my work attire and head for the elevator when I catch sight of Luka standing by the exit. He's leaning against the brick wall, his arms folded across his chest.

"What are you doing here?"

His suit looks disheveled, but I'm not sure why. There's not a scrape on his face, but I could have sworn it seems like he's been in a fight.

I glance him over as I hit the down button for the elevator and catch a glimpse of his knuckles.

Bruised.

He got into it with someone.

My stomach flops. Did he run into Mark? Is that why he doesn't look like the picture-perfect version of Luka that I'm accustomed to seeing. However, it's not like I see him often, until this past week.

"Madisyn told me what happened."

I can't believe her! I made her promise not to say anything to Luka. I should have known that she couldn't be trusted.

"Did you get Bay from preschool?" I ask. My heart quickens its pace. If he forgot to pick Bay up from school, the office should have called and informed me hours ago. No one tried to call the hospital, and my phone needs a new sim card before I can use it.

Had they tried the emergency contact? Mark's name had been placed on the sheet, but they should have known not to hand Bay over to him. I'd made it clear that his name was to be removed from the pick-up list.

The elevator doors open.

"Yes, Bay is at home with Madisyn."

"She should be in bed," I say. It's eleven o'clock at night. I step into the elevator, and Luka follows close behind. I push the button for the lobby.

"I'm sure she is," Luka says.

"You didn't tuck her into bed. How long have you been waiting out here by the elevators?"

How had I not noticed his presence? I'd changed stations, working at the opposite end of the hallway a couple of hours ago when I needed to cover for another nurse.

"I wanted to talk to you when you got off work," Luka says. He's somber.

The elevator is empty except for the two of us. "Did something happen?" I ask.

"Mark is dead."

I inhale a sharp breath, and I gasp, choking on his words. "Dead?" I can't breathe. I'm suffocating. All the air inside the elevator has been swallowed up, and I'm struggling to survive.

"Hannah, breathe," Luka says. His hands are on my arms. They're strong and warm, but he doesn't hurt me like Mark did when he grabbed me.

Luka tries to steady me.

"Breathe in."

I inhale a deep breath.

"Breathe out," Luka says.

I follow his instruction.

The elevator dings, and the doors open. My body is covered in a sheen of icy cold sweat. My heart hammers against my ribcage, and I'm gasping for air again.

"What happened?" I ask.

"You're having a panic attack," Luka says. He walks me over toward a nearby bench and guides me to sit. He stands in front of me, his legs trapping me, keeping me from falling forward if I faint.

"I meant with Mark," I say. "You said that he was dead." I can't wrap my head around what happened or how Luka would have even found out if something happened to Mark.

"Mikhail sent a couple of guys to your place to see if Mark needed a hand packing."

"Sure, he did," I say, staring up at Luka. I don't believe him. It hurts me even to ask it, but I have to know. "Did you kill him?"

Luka takes a step back, appalled by my question. "He had a heart attack, Hannah."

I press my lips together and exhale a sigh of relief. My gaze falls to my hands folded together in my lap. "He was under a lot of stress the last couple of days."

"Don't go blaming yourself for what he did to you," Luka's voice rises, and I glance around, worried that someone might overhear our conversation.

Maybe I shouldn't be ashamed of what happened, but I don't want anyone else to know to look at me the way Luka does, like I need coddling.

I'm not a child.

I can take care of myself. I've done it all my life until Luka showed up, and now what? Am I just supposed to let him handle things and help me out?

Exhaling a sigh, I rub my forehead and pull my keys out of my pocket.

It's late, and there aren't many people in the lobby. A guard is near the door, but he's too far away to hear our conversation.

"I'm sorry." I apologize for accusing Luka of doing something to Mark. Luka isn't a monster. He wouldn't hurt anyone. What kind of a person am I to think such terrible thoughts?

Luka pulls me against him. He's warm and strong, and his manly scent wafts over me. It's strangely relaxing and almost hypnotizing.

I finally untangle from his embrace. "I should head out to the garage. I'll meet you back at your place?"

"Our place," Luka says, correcting me, "and I'll drive you home." He opens his hand for me to deposit my keys into his palm.

"How'd you get here?"

"I got a ride," Luka says. "You're not driving after the news about Mark. You're in shock," he says, glancing me over.

Should I be crying? There's a heaviness that weighs on my chest and a rock in the pit of my stomach. My eyes burn, but it's not from tears. I excuse it as a lack of sleep.

There's no sense in arguing with Luka. He's trying to do the right thing, and if that means driving me back to his place, I accept the offer.

I drop my keys into his hands, and he closes his fingers around the metal and slides his arm into mine, linking us together. "Come on, lead me to the car," Luka says. "And for the record, we're not going to my house. It's our house."

I've not had enough sleep or am overly emotionally from the news Luka dropped on me about Mark's death. It was a bombshell, and it took until now to detonate.

One single statement, *it's our house,* brings me crumbling to my knees, sobbing.

Luka is calm, strong, my solid foundation as he pulls me into his arms. His hand strokes my head, and I swear I feel his strong pulse against my chest.

I soak his shirt from my tears. I don't want to cry, to grieve, to break down. Especially not while at work, but at least I made it to the lobby and not on the floor with our patients.

My chest hurts, and I don't understand why. Mark hurt me. Broke me. He betrayed my trust by pretending to be someone he wasn't, holding Bay and me against our will in the apartment.

But I was going to start a life with him, and we shared a home. Those feelings don't just vanish into thin air, even if I wish it all away.

Luka drives us back in my car to the mansion that I now call home. It's strange, living under another man's roof. It's not my home, not yet. Maybe with time, it'll feel like that when I've adjusted to the world around me.

But for the moment, I feel numb.

Frozen.

Luka escorts me into the house. I don't remember the drive home other than sitting in the front seat. The world around me has become a blur.

"Are you hungry? Did you eat dinner at work?" Luka asks. He brushes a stray lock of hair behind my ear, his attention entirely on me.

Another gentleman approaches Luka. "Can I have a word with you?"

"I'm busy at the moment, Nikita. Can it wait?"

"Find me when you have a spare moment," Nikita says and strides across the hall before heading into an office.

"What was that about?" I ask. "You work at this hour?"

"I work at every hour," Luka says and warmly smiles. His thumb strokes my jaw, and I think he might kiss me for a moment.

He doesn't.

"If you're not hungry, how about I tuck you into bed?" he asks.

"Bay is asleep," I remind him and offer him a reassuring smile that I can take care of myself. "I don't want to wake her."

His hands wrap around my waist, pulling me against him. "You could share a bed with me."

"That's probably not a great idea," I say. While the thought is tempting, I shouldn't fall into his bed to get over Mark.

He doesn't loosen his hold around my hips. His hands are firm as they lock together against my lower back. Luka's touch is relaxing but not in the fall asleep kind of way. "We don't have to sleep together," he says, staring into my gaze. "I'm told that I give great massages."

I breathe in a sharp breath, and I swear he can probably hear my heart thumping against my chest.

"Or if you're exhausted, we can just sleep," he says.

Yeah, like last night was just friends hanging out having drinks. That almost resulted in the two of us naked. Not that I regret it, but we should take things a little slower.

"As tempting as an offer, Bay will wake up and wonder where I am in the morning."

He smiles and loosens his hold. Luka isn't the least bit upset, but he's honest. "You have an excuse for everything, don't you?"

"Well, we are living together. Shouldn't we try to make this work? As co-parents." I'm trying to be a good mother for Bay, putting my daughter's needs above my desires.

"Is that what you want?" Luka asks. He walks me backward, pinning me against the wall in the hallway, trapping me.

The heat of his proximity causes my breathing to deepen.

His eyes have darkened, his mouth parts, and he leans in, his voice whispers as he grazes my ear. "We can remain professional. But I want to hear it from your lips. That what we had meant nothing and will never happen again."

"I never said it meant nothing." My head rests against the wall, and I tilt upward to glance into his fiery gaze. My lips part and I'm already raspy. The hallway is stifling, and his intense stare only heats me further. "I'm still attracted to you, Luka. That hasn't changed." I don't hide my desires or my feelings toward him. There's no reason to pretend when he can see it right in front of him.

"Why not give us a try?" he asks.

"Mark just died. Are we seriously having this conversation now?"

"All I asked was about tucking you into bed," Luka says. He doesn't so much as glance away. He rests one hand against the wall and the other on my hip.

His touch is my undoing.

Thick, rough hands stroke my hip, the pads of his fingers caress my bare skin at the hem of my shirt. My breathing is raspy, and my eyelids grow heavy.

"That's it," he whispers, pleased with my response. "Just relax."

I dip my head back, and his lips latch onto my neck, gently sucking and nibbling the skin. His fingers tease the waistband of my pants, skimming against my stomach, making my insides flutter and sending a warm pulsing sensation shooting through me.

"This isn't tucking me into bed," I rasp. I'm mouthy, and I want him to silence me by giving me what Mark couldn't. No doubt, Luka knows he's riled me up inside and is proud of his accomplishments.

The corners of his lips quirk upwards. "I suppose it's not." Luka leans closer, his lips teasing me, taunting me to kiss him. But he doesn't close the gap between us. "Do you want me to stop? Because say the word, and I'll send you upstairs to bed."

"I want you to take me up to your bed and have your way with me," I say.

Luka growls as he nips at my bottom lip, tugging it between his teeth. "I want that too, Zaya."

I whimper, and Luka thrusts his knee between my thighs, putting the perfect pressure on my center. My eyes shut, and I'm doing everything I can not to grind my hips into his knee.

But he seems to have other ideas. His knee pushes upwards until I can no longer stifle a moan. He releases a little pressure and makes the motion again and again.

Anyone could see us. One of his buddies had been in the hallway a few minutes ago. Where did he go?

"Luka," I purr, my fingernails scraping over his back, clawing at him. He's going to drive me mad with lust.

He keeps me pinned to the wall, his knee thrusting against my core, making me hot and my insides throb.

He leans forward, his lips brushing against my ear. He whispers, "You're going to come for me, *Zaya*."

I whimper.

The hallway is a thousand degrees, and I want to rip off my clothes, but anyone could walk in and see what we're doing. And while it's late and most of the house is in bed, there are men awake, walking the halls, doing whatever they do for work.

Their footsteps approach the hallway, and a shudder courses through my body.

Luka continues grinding his knee up against me. His erection pokes me, and I reach to his belt buckle, wanting to undo his slacks. I want to give him pleasure, touch him and further excite him.

"Nu-uh, this is about you," Luka says and pins my arms against the wall.

I'm in both heaven and hell. I want Luka to ravish me, but I'm not thrilled with the prospect of being seen.

"Upstairs?" I rasp.

Luka's lips tickle my neck, and he slightly pulls back, meeting my gaze. "That can be arranged." He takes my hand and leads me up to his bedroom.

The moment the door is shut, he pushes me up against the wood. Our mouths are fused with heated kisses. We'll never make it to the bed at this rate, and I don't care.

He tugs at my shirt, yanking it off, and tosses it across the room. His bedroom is dimly lit, but his fingers trace the bruises on my neck. Luka's attention is on the blemishes that Mark left behind.

"Be glad he's dead," Luka says, dropping his lips to my neck. "Anyone who lays a finger on you, I'll kill."

I inhale a sharp breath at his words. I never asked for Luka's protection or devotion. A dozen conflicting thoughts begin to race through my mind about Luka and Mark, but they're silenced when Luka shoves his mouth over mine, his tongue entering my lips.

My fingers tangle in his hair, pulling him closer and backing him up toward the bed. I need to forget the pain, erase the memories that haunt me. Luka is the only man capable of making me feel alive.

"Condom?" I ask, making sure that we're ready, although Luka is still fully dressed, and I haven't removed my pants yet.

"Slow down there, *Zaya*," Luka says and grins. He turns me around, guiding me onto the mattress.

I shift backward, and he crawls above me, his fingers rough and warm as he inches my pants down, dragging them off and tossing them behind him.

He climbs between my legs and places one leg on his shoulder as he leans in towards my panties, nuzzling the thin fabric. "You're wet for me," he says, pleased with his accomplishments.

He teases me through the flimsy material, and I swear I feel his tongue. The barrier of cotton is too thick.

He senses my discomfort and rips my panties off, making my stomach flutter. "You look so fucking sexy naked," Luka whispers. He gently guides my leg back down to the mattress as he climbs atop me.

"I want to see you naked."

"And you will," Luka says, smiling down at me. His eyes shine, and my heart hammers in my chest.

I reach for his shirt, yanking the white cotton open, the buttons tearing away.

"That was my good shirt," Luka says pointedly, pressing my arms into the mattress.

"Seriously? Every shirt you wear looks the same." I've only been around him a handful of days, but he always dresses the same. I'll bet every dress shirt in his closet is white.

He growls playfully and leans down, capturing my lips as he presses his weight against me.

I can't help the moan that spills past my lips as I wrap my legs around him. Instead, I'm not fighting for control but want to fuel his desire. I wrestle his hips, trying to flip us around so I can properly undress him.

But Luka has other ideas that don't involve me dominating him.

"Have you ever been tied up in bed?" Luka asks, his lips caressing my ear.

My mouth goes dry. The idea has intrigued me, but I don't know Luka well enough to trust him, to give myself over to him completely. That's a huge step. "It's a fantasy," I confess and chew on my bottom lip. "But not for today."

He drops another heated kiss to my lips and releases his grip on my arms.

My hands reach out, grazing his chest, touching his bare skin as I let my fingers wander down to his belt buckle. I free the clip, and he unzips his pants, allowing me to remove his pants and boxers as I admire every inch of him.

"You're staring," he says.

How can I not? He's enormous, well-endowed, and puts Mark to shame. Not that Mark was good at sex.

I let my fingers drift past his stomach as I reach for my intended destination, but Luka grabs my wrists and pushes me back against the mattress. "Remember, tonight is about you."

"Yes, and I want to taste you," I say, glancing down, although I can't see much between us pressed against the mattress.

He's trying to hide the smile, but his eyes shine. "You will, the next time we do this," Luka says.

My heart slams against my ribcage at his admission that this isn't a one-time thing happening between us, that he wants this to occur again.

The room is warm, and I'm confident that I'm flushed or at the very least blushing.

"Relax, *Zaya*." He releases his firm grip against my arms and drops fervent kisses over my skin, from my neck down my torso.

Each kiss makes me restless for more with him.

It's like he knows exactly what I need and gives it to me, again and again. His mouth is warm and teases my inner thighs with a soft trail of kisses.

I inhale a sharp breath as he finally reaches his intended destination, and it's a million times better than I imagined with Luka.

He drags his tongue over my pussy, and my insides quake and shudder as he tastes, teases, and brings me toward oblivion.

Luka knows precisely what to do, and my heart pounds against my chest, my toes curl, and my back arches up off the mattress.

He crawls back up my torso after the first wave ripples through me and kisses me as he grabs a condom. He inches his cock inside my warmth a moment later, confident that I'm ready for him.

Luka fills every inch of me, making my insides ache in the most delicious way possible.

The room fills with moans and heavy breaths, gasping for air, panting, as he thrusts inside me. I wrap my legs around him, drawing him deeper, wanting him closer, tighter, and one with me.

Another wave comes crashing down, and he bites my neck, leaving a delicious mark. I shudder and moan, and Luka covers my lips with his. I can't tell if he's silencing me because I'll wake the entire house or he's as needy as I am, wanting to be tangled with him.

I don't want the moment ever to end, but when it does, he drops a kiss to my forehead and climbs off to dispose of the condom.

I reach for the covers, exhausted. Is he going to ask me to return to my room? I should, because Bay is in there, and otherwise, come morning, she will be upset when she wakes up alone in a relatively unfamiliar home.

But instead, I shut my eyes.

The bathroom light is turned off, and the bed dips as Luka climbs under the covers with me. He pulls me against him, spooning me.

"I never took you for a cuddler," I mumble, half-asleep.

"I'm not," Luka whispers against my neck. "Not usually. Enjoying the time that I have with you in my bed."

EIGHTEEN

Luka

There's a firm knock on the bedroom door.

I overslept. One glance at the clock, and it's well past eight. Not that I care. I reach beside me, and the bed is ice cold. Hannah must have sneaked out this morning or sometime during the night.

I didn't hear her leave.

"Just a sec!" I call and grab my boxers, slipping them on before opening the bedroom door.

Nikita is dressed and ready to face the day.

Me? I'd prefer to climb back into bed with a sexy brunette downstairs.

"What's up?" I ask and rub the back of my neck.

Nikita nods. "Can I come in?"

I open the bedroom door, and he glances around, taking note of my clothes flung around the room. "Hot date with the mom downstairs?" The grin on his face tells me he's not going to keep it a secret.

"What do you want, Nikita?"

"I've got the information that Mikhail asked for about Mark. Once I managed to get his full name, Markus Jacobi, I realized the connection pretty quickly. He's one of ours," Nikita says.

"That can't be," I say, shaking my head. I'd have recognized Mark if he worked for the bratva. While I don't know every soldier and associate, I'm good with faces and names.

"He was a low-level associate, Markus Jacobi. He oversaw the books for one of the clubs Mikhail owns."

I bend down, picking up my clothes from the night before, including a half dozen buttons strewn about the floor. "Hannah mentioned that he was an accountant."

"From what I can tell, he was skimming money, just a little bit every month, into an off-seas account in the Caymans. It seems he realized that he was involved in a money-laundering scheme and decided to help himself to a cut of our share."

"Dumbass," I mutter. "Who knew about the theft?"

"Mark has been working with Dmitri," Nikita says. "Dmitri suspected Mark was dirty and had Anton put surveillance on his office but not his home."

"Who else knew?"

"The team who set up the electronic surveillance. Dmitri didn't even tell Mikhail because he didn't want to worry him if he was wrong. You know how quick Mikhail can be to react. Dmitri didn't want to jump to conclusions. He didn't have evidence, just suspicion."

"But Mikhail didn't recognize Mark the other night," I say. We roughed him up pretty good outside of the compound. Shouldn't he have known one of his employees?

"Mikhail hadn't met directly with Mark, and he knew him as Markus. There'd be no reason for

Mikhail to realize Hannah's fiancé was our accountant."

I grab my clothes from the closet and head into the bathroom, listening to Nikita through the door. "How much does Hannah know about Mark's involvement?"

"That's why I'm here, knocking on your door," Nikita says. "I had to report what I found to Mikhail first. He wants to know if your girl can be trusted."

I change boxers and pull on my pants before I open the door. "Hannah doesn't know anything," I say. I grab a crisp white shirt and slide it on over my shoulders, working on the buttons from the top down.

"Are you sure? What about the Cayman account?" Nikita asks.

"I'll ask her, but she might have more questions about our business when I do."

————

Bay is seated on the floor, playing with the stuffed animals we brought from the house.

Hannah is on the floor with her, pretending to have a tea party with the entire zoo.

"Can we sit down and talk?" I ask Hannah.

"Sure," she says and stands. "I'll be right back. Stay here, okay?" Hannah drops a kiss to Bay's forehead before following me out of the study, down the hallway, and into my office.

She steps foot inside and glances around the room. "What's going on?" She folds her arms across her chest. I can't tell if she's cold or uncomfortable.

"Have a seat," I gesture to the leather chair, and she frowns but does as I instruct.

"Luka? Are you regretting last night?" Her brow is furrowed, and I want to assure her that last night has nothing to do with my questions, but I can't comfort her now.

There's a sharp knock on the door and Mikhail steps inside the office.

He wants to watch the interrogation, although I don't plan on it being a full-scale inquiry. As far as I'm concerned, Hannah hasn't done anything wrong.

Mikhail stands by the door, hands folded together in front of him. He nods at me to do the talking and to begin.

"Did you know that Mark worked for Mikhail?"

She glances from me over her shoulder at the pakhan. "No. He never mentioned it." She rubs her forehead, and her attention returns to me. "He has a lot of important clients. I don't know any of them. What is this about?"

"Your fiancé stole money from me," Mikhail says. He struts farther into the office, coming to stand beside me. "We believe that he created an off-shore account in the Cayman Islands where he transferred a percentage of our funds."

Hannah's eyes widen, and she sits back in the leather chair. Her face is ghastly. "This is news to me. Mark was practically a saint up until this week."

I exchange a glance with Mikhail.

"What do you mean?" Mikhail asks, wanting a further explanation of events.

She sighs, and her shoulders slump as she stares up at me. "It all started when I ran into Luka at the bar with Madisyn. When Luka brought me home, he ran into Mark at the front door. Things changed. Mark changed."

I glance at Mikhail. "It's possible Markus recognized me." The bratva owns his workplace, and while he has an office of his own in our facility, we could have easily crossed paths.

"What do you mean, recognized you?" Hannah stands and glances between us. "I don't know what's going on, but Mark is dead. Do you want access to the account overseas? I can comb through the apartment and see if I find any account information," Hannah says.

"That isn't necessary," Mikhail says, glancing her over. He's studying her, making sure that she's not lying to him or hiding something of further importance. "We can trace his computer and find the money ourselves."

It's not as easy as it sounds, but Mikhail doesn't let on that it is a lengthy endeavor to track down the funds.

Hannah nods slowly. "I'm sorry about his betrayal to your company." The corners of her lips are turned downward. "He never talked about his job or his clients with me."

"He only had one client," Mikhail says. He glances at me and then back at Hannah. "Would you give us a minute?"

She stands from the chair and heads toward the door. "You said he had one client?" Hannah asks as she approaches the door.

"That's right," Mikhail says. "We've kept him busy with our paperwork and finances."

"He mentioned moving overseas for work. That wasn't true, was it?" Hannah exhales a soft breath, her bottom lip pouts.

"He wouldn't have been moving regarding his job," I say. Mark planned on running and moving to the Caymans after siphoning enough money for a fresh start. Men like Markus who steal from the bratva have a short shelf-life. He must have known that we were on to him. "Go keep Bay company. I'll come to get you if we have any further questions."

Hannah heads out of my office, quietly closing the door behind herself.

I wait until she's not outside the door and down the hallway. "I believe her," I say, waiting for Mikhail's input. His view is the only one that matters, but I want it stated that I don't believe Hannah has done anything wrong.

"Based on the surveillance footage that Nikita showed me from the office, Markus didn't contact her or anyone else while at work. Her story sounds legit. Keep an eye on her around the compound and make sure she's not trying to get any information, but I have no reason to suspect her involvement."

I breathe a sigh of relief. It's good that Hannah's not on Mikhail's radar, because if she were, she'd probably be thrown downstairs into the prison and interrogated with far harsher methods than sitting down for a little chat.

Mikhail heads out of the office, and I sit down at my desk to finish going through the surveillance footage that we took and erase the video of the night of Mark's death.

There's a rough knock at the door. "Come in," I say to whoever is on the other side.

Madisyn steps foot inside my office. She closes the door behind herself.

"What's going on?" I ask.

"We need to talk."

NINETEEN

Hannah

A Few Minutes Earlier...

Mark lied to me. This week just keeps getting better and better. First, he held me against my will in the apartment. Then, he had a heart attack and died. Now, I'm discovering that he stole money from the company who employed him.

"Mama," Bay says and shoves the play teapot at me to refill. It's pretend tea, make-believe, but my mind is a million miles away, and I'm too distracted to remember how to make fake tea.

Bay climbs into my lap when I'm not doing what she wants quickly.

There's a heavy set of footsteps trailing down the hallway, and I glance at the door as a gentleman I don't recognize steps into the study. "Ma'am, this was found with the laundry. I believe it got mixed up accidentally in the clothes bin." He hands me a red envelope, sealed.

My name is scribbled on the front in Mark's handwriting.

"Where did you get this?" I ask, chasing after the gentleman and sitting Bay on the floor.

"As I said, the laundry. One of the housekeepers found it in with the clothes and thought it should be returned to you."

"Thank you," I say, studying the envelope.

He hurries back to his duties, disappearing down the hallway. I've seen the gentleman once or twice, but I never caught his name.

Exhaling a nervous breath, I'm not sure if I'm ready to read the letter. What if it's an apology?

Doubtful.

It's probably a letter Mark wrote me about how I'm a terrible person leaving him and how I'll never be happy without him in my life. I shouldn't open the envelope. Instead, I should shove it into the nearest paper shredder or burn it.

But curiosity gets the best of me, and I tear open the envelope, pulling out a handwritten note from Mark.

Hannah,

I wish I could explain everything in person. But I can't. Not while you're living under the roof of the bratva.

I warned you to stay away from Luka and not to tell him that Bay is his biological kin. I can't protect you if you're with him. And while I wanted to tell you everything, telling you could get you killed.

Luka is not the man he claims to be. He's a liar. Has he told you that he works for Mikhail Barinov, the biggest crime boss on the east coast?

I only know this because I work for him. I never met the man; he is too smart to let his hands get dirty. But there's evidence, a paper trail from his illicit dealings.

Luka is Russian Bratva. They're powerful and dangerous men who would kill me to keep you from discovering the truth.

If I end up dead, you should know that I may not have been innocent, but neither are they. They're murderers, thieves, drug lords, and felons.

Be careful.

Mark

My breath catches in my throat, and I read the letter once more, making sure I'm not missing anything. I shove the envelope and the contents into my pocket.

We can't stay here. If Mark was right and Luka is part of a crime organization, Bay isn't safe with Luka.

I grab Bay from the floor.

"Mama, down!" Bay proclaims as I reach for her favorite stuffed rabbit and hand it to her to preoccupy her while I hurry down the hallway past Luka's office.

I can't confront him. He'd only lie to me. A man working for the bratva will not admit to his nefarious acts.

I hurry down the hallway, searching for Madisyn. She's in the kitchen, grabbing a snack from the fridge.

"We have to get out of here," I say, keeping my voice down.

Madisyn opens a Ben & Jerry's ice cream tub and takes a spoonful, shoving the sweet treat into her mouth. She's staring at me like I've gone mad.

I wish that I had. It would be easier to deal with than knowing that the father of my child is a monster.

"Huh?" Madisyn asks, waiting for a further explanation for my outburst.

I show her the envelope and letter, slightly crinkled but still entirely legible. "Mikhail, Luka, they're bratva," I say. I glance behind us at the open entryway to the kitchen. "I'm getting out of here with Bay. You should come with us," I say, glancing her over.

She's not visibly pregnant, at least I can't see it, but she can't want this life for her child.

"I'm not leaving," Madisyn says. "And I think you should talk to Luka before you jet." She takes another bite of ice cream, not upset by the news.

"Did you know they're bratva?" I can't believe that she wouldn't have told me. How is she okay with this for her child?

"I used to work for the FBI," Madisyn says.

She told me that once before, but I didn't believe her. I thought that she was joking about being a federal agent.

I back out of the kitchen. "I can't stay." I hurry down the hallway and for the front door. I don't bother packing anything. There's no time.

I put Bay into the backseat and buckle her into her booster seat before I climb into the front seat, slam the door, and head out. Thankfully, the guard opens the gate without so much as a question.

At least we're not prisoners. I breathe a sigh of relief, but I don't feel calm or comforted. I can't return to work. Luka knows where I used to live, work, and everything about me.

I have to head out of the city, away from New York, to safety. It's the only chance to keep Bay and me safe.

TWENTY

Luka

There's a forceful knock at the door. "Come in," I say.

Madisyn slowly opens the door to my office and pokes her head in. I gesture for her to step inside, and my stomach flips when I see the red envelope from last night, which Mark had left for Hannah.

"Where did you get that?" I ask. I can see the contents torn open upon further inspection, although I don't know what the letter said. I never read it.

"Hannah gave it to me. She wanted me to leave with her."

"Leave?" I leap up from my desk and brush past Madisyn. "Did you let her leave?" I head for the study where Bay had been playing earlier in the afternoon.

"I'm not her keeper," Madisyn says as she follows me down the hallway. She folds her arms across her chest when I glance into the study and see the toys abandoned but no sign of Hannah or Bay.

"Where did she go?"

"You should have been honest with her," Madisyn says. "She was going to find out eventually. What did you think would happen when she discovered the truth from her ex-fiancé?"

I sneer at her suggestion. "He wasn't supposed to tell her. He's dead!"

Mikhail steps out of his office, hearing the commotion. "What the hell is going on out here?"

"Hannah left with Bay," I say. "She found out that we're bratva and took off with my kid."

"Bay is her kid too," Madisyn says. "She's just trying to protect her. She'll come back."

I glare at Madisyn. "You don't know Hannah. She's not coming back." I head toward the garage and grab a set of keys.

"Where are you going?" Mikhail asks. "Unless you know where she's going, you'll never find her."

That's the point. She doesn't want to be found. Hannah doesn't have a cell phone that I can track, and I never put a GPS tracker on her vehicle.

"I can't just let her leave with my daughter!" I run my fingers through my hair. "What do you suggest I do?"

"We can hack into surveillance footage of roadways and follow her vehicle to wherever she goes," Mikhail says. He's calm. Like he's done this before and is not the least bit concerned.

Sweat beads at my forehead. My stomach is in knots, and I'm hoping not to get sick. Maybe I shouldn't care, but Bay is my daughter, and if Hannah wants to leave, Bay stays in my custody.

"Have a seat in my office," Mikhail says, and I do as he asks.

My skin is crawling, and my leg bounces, antsy to do something. I'm not a man who sits still and waits. Everything inside of me aches with the knowledge that she's gone, and it's because she's angry with me.

How could I not have seen it coming?

"Just sit tight. Let me find Nikita," Mikhail says and hustles out of his office and down the hallway. He leaves the door open.

Madisyn stands by the door. "I'm sorry," she says, her hands clasped together. Her apology is sincere, but it doesn't remove the pain or ease what happened.

Will I ever see Hannah and Bay again?

Even if I find them, how am I going to fix this? I'm bratva. It's a part of who I am. I can't just walk away from it, even if I wanted to leave.

I exhale a heavy sigh and lean forward, my head in my hands. I royally fucked up. "Just when things were finally going right," I mutter.

"It can be fixed," Madisyn says. She leans against the doorjamb and folds her arms across her chest.

"How?" I glare up at her.

"Explain it to her," Madisyn says. She's calm, but she knew from the beginning that Mikhail was the leader of the bratva.

"I don't think a bouquet of roses and an apology will fix this situation."

"Chocolates," Madisyn quips with a grin.

I'm not smiling. "It's not funny." How can she laugh? Oh right, it's not her kid's life that was whisked away. "I blame you."

"Me? What did I do?" Madisyn scoffs and steps farther into the office, standing in front of me.

"You're friends with Hannah."

"And?" she stares down at me. "What's that have to do with anything? I didn't introduce the two of you."

I clench my jaw, ignoring her as she hovers and steals my personal space. "Back off," I snarl, wanting space and to be left alone.

"Fine," Madisyn huffs under and stomps off like a little kid.

There is no easy way to fix what happened. Groveling isn't my strong suit. I'm usually direct and take what I want, but Hannah isn't going to fall back into my arms because I tell her I want her in my life.

As I sit in silence, Mikhail doesn't return for quite some time, tracking down Anton and giving him orders to hack the traffic cameras. I didn't realize he could hack anything, but maybe he's reaching out to the associate who handles that type of work.

My phone buzzes with an alert. I yank my phone from my jacket pocket, unsure what to expect. Most of the alerts on my phone are on silent, like texts and emails. The notification alerts me that there is motion at the apartment.

Hannah's apartment.

"What the hell?" I open the application and get a live feed of Hannah and Bay in the living room of the apartment.

Thankfully, Mark's body was removed, and evidence of our involvement was cleaned up.

I turn on the audio feed, making sure not to turn on the microphone so she can't hear me. "What is she doing?" I say, watching her scrounge through the apartment.

We grabbed a bunch of clothes already and toys for Bay.

Hannah isn't packing anything. It's like she's looking for something.

I can't sit around and watch, waiting to see where she goes next. I hurry out of Mikhail's office, breezing by him in the hallway. "She's at her apartment," I say, rushing toward the garage to grab the car keys.

"What's she doing there?" Mikhail asks.

"Hell if I know, but I'm taking it as a win." I just have to get there before she finds whatever she's looking for and leaves.

I hurry across town, blowing through several traffic lights and stop signs to get to Hannah's apartment before she's gone.

I run up the stairs, not waiting for the elevator. It's only three flights of stairs. As I approach the door, I raise my hand and give a firm knock.

Will she run?

She won't take Bay down the fire escape, and the windows are too high to sneak out.

There's movement on the opposite side of the door, but she doesn't come and open the door or see who's knocking.

I try the handle, but it's locked. Maybe I shouldn't be surprised, but I pound again on the door louder. "Hannah, we need to talk."

Her footsteps are loud as she approaches the door, unlocks the latch, and tugs the door open. "What do you want?"

"Can I come in, or do you want your neighbors to hear everything?"

Hannah's gaze tightens, but she steps aside. Her lips are pursed, and she folds her arms across her chest. "Bay, sweetie, go in your bedroom for a few minutes."

"Don't want to," Bay whines, staring at me. "Mama's mad at you."

Yeah, kid, tell me something I don't already know. I bend down to Bay's level. "How about you listen to your mom?" I ruffle her hair, and she wiggles out of my grasp before running to her bedroom.

"Whatever you came here to say, I don't want to hear it," Hannah says. She turns her back to me and continues the assault on her apartment, pulling drawers open and tearing the place apart.

"What are you looking for?" Does she have cash stored away or a second set of papers and documents to hide from me?

"The stupid account that you claim Mark has in the Caymans," Hannah says. "If I find you the account information, will you leave Bay and me alone?"

"I don't care about the money."

Mikhail might disagree with me, but it's not about the money with Hannah. It's about my child. I want Bay in my life. Doesn't she realize that?

She glances over her shoulder at me as she tears apart the computer desk. Each drawer is on the floor. She's searching for a false bottom, but I doubt Mark would hide the evidence in his desk. That would be too obvious, even for him. "Why are you here?" Hannah asks.

"I never wanted you to leave."

"And the letter?" Her back is to me once again. She doesn't want to face me. I can feel her anger, maybe even resentment, for trusting me.

"I never opened it. I may have put it into my coat pocket, but that's all I did."

She scoffs at my suggestion that I'm innocent in all of this. "You took it from my apartment and didn't tell me."

It's not a question but an accusation.

"I should have told you," I say, refraining from making excuses.

"Did you plan on giving it to me?" Hannah asks, spinning around to face me.

The envelope is in my pocket, the contents burn me as she speaks about it, and I slowly withdraw the letter and envelope from my jacket. It's open, crinkled, but still legible. "There was no malice involved, *Zaya.*"

"Don't call me that!" She snatches the letter from my grasp. "This doesn't belong to you."

She's right, the letter was intended for her, and while I took it to protect her, I understand that she doesn't see it that way.

No amount of apologizing will help, and I'm not a man who begs for forgiveness. "You can hate me all you want, but I have the right to see my daughter."

She's shaking her head, her cheeks red. She's fiery and about to explode like a volcano. I should take a step back, retreat, find common ground, and put this fight off for another day.

But I'm not a man to back down or turn away from difficult situations. I deal with them daily, although they don't usually involve my family.

"You have no right, Luka!" Hannah shouts at me.

I step closer, sealing the gap between us, breaking the distance as I tower above her. A smart man would know to give her space, but I'm more interested in the fire in her gaze. She will break, and when she does, I will be the one to pick up the pieces, even if it means tearing her down first.

"I'm her father. The court will say differently."

Her jaw drops, and she shoves me as she brushes past me and heads toward the kitchen.

"Go ahead, take me to court. I'll show them the evidence that you're involved with organized crime. You'll never see Bay again."

"You're bluffing. You don't have anything." I follow her into the kitchen, backing her up against the counter. "If you did, don't you think the feds or cops would be knocking on my door? Is that why you came back here? Looking for dirt on me?"

Hannah inhales a sharp breath and shivers.

The room isn't cold except for her icy stare as she sneers at me. "I hate you."

"Tell me what I've done to deserve your abhorrence?" I tilt my head slightly, staring down at her.

Her back is against the island in the kitchen. She glances past me, her tongue darts out, grazing the edge of her lips.

"*Zaya*?" I'm awaiting her answer. Perhaps I should remind her of everything I've done for her, helping her and protecting her and our child. "I offered you shelter, a home, safety from a man who imprisoned you."

She opens her lips, and a heavy sigh escapes. "That's harsh."

"Am I wrong?"

Hannah can't meet my stare. She knows I'm right. I reach up and rest my thumb under her chin, guiding her gaze toward me. "He bruised you, broke you, and you think I'm the monster?"

"You're a criminal," Hannah says. There's a glint of fear behind her blue eyes. She's afraid of me. What have I done to deserve her fear and disgust?

I won't talk about my crimes, certainly not under her roof. The cameras are still functioning and recording. Anyone could intercept the signal, including the FBI.

While I haven't seen her run to them, I can't be certain they're not watching. Madisyn has ties to the FBI, and while she may have left that life behind, who is to say they've left us behind?

"You fear me for all the wrong reasons," I say.

She exhales a heavy huff, and her brow tightens. Hannah drags her bottom lip between her teeth, a nervous habit I catch her doing far too often. Recently, her frustration had been at Mark, which I could deal with, but Hannah despising me is something entirely new, and I don't like it.

"Really? All the wrong reasons? Tell me Mark is wrong, and you're not bratva."

I won't lie to her. Hannah deserves the truth.

Silence is my admission of guilt. I drop my hand from her jaw. Her heated stare is enough to make my stomach turn. I don't need to force her to look at me.

"Did you kill Mark too?"

"I didn't have to kill him. He dropped dead in the living room." It's the truth. Maybe I didn't help resuscitate him, but that's not a crime. The man deserved to die, and I was just lucky it happened when it did, before he could hurt Hannah again.

"I don't believe you," Hannah says.

I should take a step back and give her some space, but I don't. At least with her body trapped against the island, I know that she isn't going anywhere. She can't run while I have her within my grasp.

And she doesn't push me away.

"I can prove it to you," I say.

It's a gamble, revealing the surveillance footage. We did come to the apartment to rough up Mark. But the heart attack, that wasn't on us. I didn't kill him.

Her eyes flicker. "How?" She glances me over. Her shoulders are straight and back. Her posture is an attempt to make her look tougher and bolder, not the least bit fragile.

"After you agreed to move in with me, we had the apartment under surveillance. We wanted to make sure that Mark packed his belongings and left."

"There's video footage of my apartment?" Her hands reach my chest, and she pushes me back, scooting away from the counter as she searches for the cameras.

They're impossible to notice. High-tech and top-level equipment that government agencies use across the world. It didn't come cheap, but there is no price too high for my family's safety.

I retrieve my cell phone from my pocket and open the application. I'm honestly not sure showing her the footage is in my best interest. She wasn't aware that I was at her apartment when Mark had a heart attack, but her thinking I'm the reason he died because I murdered him, that idea needs to be nixed.

I skip past the part where I enter and shove a gun against Mark's head and bloody his nose. She doesn't need to witness the violence. I press play and hand her my phone.

She gasps and glances in the direction of one of the cameras back to the phone as the scene unfolds.

I take a tentative step back.

"Mama?" Bay pokes her head out of the bedroom.

"Get back in your room, Bay!" Hannah scolds her daughter, pointing in the direction of the little girl's bedroom.

Bay doesn't budge. She stands in her overalls with pigtails. Her shoes have since been discarded, along with her socks. Bay must have removed those items while in her bedroom.

"It's boring," she says as she stomps toward me with a huge grin. "I want my toys."

Hannah pauses the video as Bay approaches, ensuring that she doesn't witness the same event that Hannah is watching on the screen.

I bend down to Bay's level and tickle her.

"Daddy!" she squeals and wiggles into my arms.

I wrap my arms around the little tiger, hugging her.

Hannah shuts off the screen on my phone, having seen enough. She hands me back my cell phone. I'm not sure the video convinced her that I'm not the bad guy she believes me to be.

"Bay, come here," Hannah says.

"No!" the little one shouts.

Bay wraps her arms around my neck, and I glance at Hannah. "You should listen to your mother." While I don't want to let Bay go, I'm not about to kidnap my child, either.

I untangle Bay from around my neck, and Hannah steps forward, snatching Bay from the floor and picking her up. "I want the cameras removed."

"I'll have the men who installed the cameras remove them," I say.

"And I want everything returned to me in your possession, seeing as there's no reason for Bay and me to reside with you anymore."

I shove my cell phone into my jacket pocket. "Just because Mark is gone, you don't have to leave the compound."

"Compound?" Hannah repeats. "Wow. And here I thought it was just a really nice house that Mikhail owned. That's why you live there full-time, to protect his assets and property."

I ignore her remark. She's angry that I kept what I do a secret, but how could I tell her without risking her safety?

Doesn't she realize all I've wanted is to keep her safe?

"You should go," Hannah says.

I won't overstay my welcome, not that I was truly invited into her home. "Don't think that I won't fight for custody of my daughter."

Her eyes flinch. "Luka, please." Her voice cracks, and I see the resolve breaking. If I take Bay away from her, she will never forgive me.

"You can't ask me to walk away and not see my child."

Hannah heads to the door, indicating that it's time for me to leave.

"We're not having this conversation," Hannah says.

"Fine, if you won't have it now, we'll get lawyers and the court involved."

"Please, don't," she whispers.

I open the door. I'm not ready to leave, and I don't trust that she won't take off and run. If she's afraid that I'll fight for custody, it gives her motive to vanish with my daughter.

While cameras are already inside the apartment, it doesn't help me track Hannah or locate her when she steps foot outside.

I can request one of our guards watch the apartment and follow Hannah when she leaves, but for how long?

"You may not believe it, but I've already fallen madly in love with Bay. You can't keep her from me."

Hannah softly shuts the door, allowing us to talk. She puts Bay down as the kid wiggles and fidgets to break free.

The little tiger slams into my legs, practically knocking me over, giggling before deciding it's a good idea to climb me like a tree.

Hannah's shoulders slump. "I don't want this to be a custody battle, Luka."

"Neither do I. I'm not fighting you for full custody. I don't even want this to be a fight," I clarify. "Come back to the house with me, let us work through whatever is going on and figure out our relationship together."

She folds her arms across her chest. "Aside from the fact you lied to me, is it even safe for us to live with you?"

She'll be a million times safer living with me under Mikhail's roof, with armed guards and a former FBI agent living on the premises, than an apartment across town that could easily be broken into.

"Our guards are trained at keeping everyone inside the premises safe. Madisyn used to be an FBI agent. Do you think she'd live with Mikhail and bring a child into the house if it wasn't safe?"

Hannah's quiet, mulling over my words as she glances in the direction of the hallway. "You honestly didn't hurt Mark?" she asks. "Because you were there, you saw what happened."

She must not have watched the footage in its entirety. I certainly didn't show her the video of us entering the premises.

"We called the paramedics," I say. It's the truth, and if she watched the footage, she'd see that we eventually called for help. It may not have been when Mark collapsed onto the ground, but we did call for an ambulance. "Come home, Hannah, let me show you the man I am."

"Other than a monster?"

"I never claimed to be something that I'm not. You came to me for help with Mark."

She glances down at the ground. " I was running to Madisyn. I didn't know you'd be there."

"Have I ever hurt you?" I ask, pinning her with my stare.

"No, I barely know you."

That isn't my fault. She can't blame me for not finding me sooner. "What do you want to know?" I ask.

"Have you ever killed a person?"

Why does she have to start with the difficult questions?

"I've been in a war, *Zaya*. Whether it's with the bratva or for my country, men die. I'm not proud of the atrocities I've been forced to endure, but I can't erase my past, either."

Has that satisfied her nagging curiosity?

"You're dangerous," she whispers, staring at me.

She fears what she doesn't know, not who I truly am. "Come home, let me show you who I am. Don't put words into my mouth about who you think I am because that's what you've read or seen in movies. Have I ever hurt you physically? Have I laid a finger on you?"

Hannah is silent as she realizes I'm not the beast she's made me out to be.

"Mark was more of a monster than me, not because he was skimming money from us but because of what he did to you. The bruises may go away, but Mark left behind scars that need time to heal."

Bay pushes my cheeks together like a fish, squishing my face and giggling. The kid seems oblivious to the tension between us, or maybe she's trying to make everything better.

I give her props if it's the latter.

There's a heavy silence that falls over us. Hannah has to know that I'm right, that all I've wanted was to protect her and my child.

"Don't ever lie to me again," Hannah says.

TWENTY-ONE

Hannah

Luka is ready to head home. "You can leave. I'll meet you back at the compound," I say.

He shoots me a look, and I ignore it. I'm still searching for whatever account paperwork Mark must have left behind.

"That's not going to happen," Luka says.

My original plan had been to offer the account with the money to Mikhail and his men. In exchange, they would leave Bay and me alone.

But that doesn't seem likely. Luka is determined to keep Bay in his life, and I see his point. She's already smitten with him, and he is her biological father.

It's what I've wanted, his involvement in her life—in our lives.

But his involvement with organized crime doesn't quell my nerves or anxiety. How am I supposed to look the other way? What about the safety of my daughter? I could never live with myself if something happened to her.

"Then give me a hand," I say.

"What exactly are we looking for?" he asks and puts Bay down on the sofa. She climbs off and latches herself to his legs. They are inseparable, and it's only been a few days.

"Daddy." Bay clutches onto his legs, and he lifts her into the air, flipping her upside down before putting her back on the sofa. "Again."

"Again?" Luka asks, giving Bay his undivided attention. He's smiling, his eyes bright, and it's honest and genuine. Without a doubt, he loves my daughter—his daughter.

It's as though Bay has realized what she's missed out on and is making up for it, stealing his attention every second that she gets. She's too young to understand why he wasn't around, and leaving would inevitably hurt her.

I don't want that for Bay, and dare I admit that, I don't want Luka out of our lives, either. I just need stability. I can't constantly be looking over my shoulder, worried about the danger we might face because there are men who want him dead.

I hope I'm wrong, and it's nothing more than my fears and insecurities standing in the way of what could be.

"Hannah?"

"Oh, right." I've already combed through the desk, coffee table, and television console. The bedrooms drawers were also empty. "If Mark stole money from Mikhail and has a foreign account, wouldn't there be paperwork?"

Luka lifts Bay into the air, flipping her again before letting her gracefully fall onto the plush sofa. "It could also be on a laptop, thumb drive, or cloud server. There's no reason he would have had to print the documents unless he planned on wanting copies because he would flee the country."

"He mentioned us moving because of his job." I pinch the bridge of my nose. My head is throbbing, and I could use a heavy dose of caffeine to ward off an oncoming migraine.

"Maybe he did print the documents. Where does he keep his passport?" Luka asks.

"The top drawer in his desk but the passports and papers weren't there. Mine are gone too," I say.

His jaw clenches, and he is as grumpy as he looks.

"What is it?" I ask. My stomach sinks. What does he know?

"Could be nothing. I'll call Mikhail and have one of his men check the office where Mark used to work."

"Why?"

"You might have been adamant about not wanting to leave the country, but I suspect that Mark planned to flee and take the two of you with him."

I'm done searching the apartment if Luka doesn't think what he needs is in this place. I plop down onto the sofa. "Why take the documents to the office? What purpose would that serve?"

"He may have needed them to book plane tickets out of the country. Of course, he could have just taken a photograph with his phone to capture the information, but no one said Mark was smart."

Luka places Bay on the sofa beside me, and she climbs into my lap. The girl has an endless amount of energy. At least while I'm at work, she's usually at preschool and is socializing with other kids her age.

"How about we head home?" Luka says.

While his place hasn't quite felt like home to me, the cold apartment brings back memories of Mark's threats and his recent death on the living room floor.

And while I had only imagined it before, a glimpse at the video is enough to give me nightmares.

I can't live here.

"Okay," I say and lift Bay, glancing down at her bare feet. "Where are your shoes and socks, little miss?"

"I'm a tiger," Bay says, showing me her most enormous roar and hand gesture to prove her toughness.

"Did you teach her that?" I chuckle, glancing at Luka as he follows me into her bedroom and grabs her shoes and socks from the floor.

"I may have endeared her with the nickname tiger."

"And what about me? What does *Zaya* mean?" I ask. I'm confident it's a term of endearment. I just haven't figured out quite what it means.

Luka smirks, his eyes bright and twinkling with mirth. "I can't give away all of my secrets."

TWENTY-TWO

Hannah

Several Months Later...

"Oh shit!" Madisyn's voice carries down the hallway of Steele Concierge Medical.

I hurry around the corner, and before I can ask her what's wrong, I realize that she's in labor. The floor at her feet is shiny and wet. Her water broke.

"I need you to call Mikhail," Madisyn orders between contractions. I don't have Mikhail's phone number on my phone, and now doesn't seem like a grand time to ask for it, either.

She's focusing on her breathing, and I'm taking her downstairs to labor and delivery. The surgical unit is no place for a woman to give birth, and I may be a nurse, but I'm not about to catch Madisyn's newborn.

I've memorized Luka's phone number, and the minute I step into the elevator, he picks up the call.

"Hello?"

"Is Mikhail with you?"

"Yes," Luka says. "Why? What's wrong?" His cheery hello has turned to concern.

"Nothing," I say, not wanting to worry him.

"It's not nothing!" Madisyn shrieks as she grasps the elevator wall, and the reception on the phone gets spotty.

I pull back the phone to see if I've lost the call. Not yet, but it's hard to hear anything. As soon as we get to the ground floor and the double doors open, Luka is back on the line.

"Madisyn is in labor," I say.

"I got that from her screaming," Luka says. "We're on our way to the hospital. Stay with her until we get there."

Where else am I going to go?

"Can you swing by and pick up Bay from preschool?" I ask.

"After I drop off Mikhail at the hospital," Luka says. "We're already in the car and halfway there."

I don't bother to ask what they were up to; I know better than to discuss their business dealings.

I don't want to know. That's the agreement that we made. He'd keep his business responsibilities to himself to protect Bay and me.

Although he swears that I worry too much.

And he might be right.

Madisyn is whisked away by a nurse, and I follow down the hall, refusing to leave her side. "Do you want to talk to Mikhail?" I ask, giving her privacy while she's behind a curtain with the nurse, helping her change into a hospital gown.

"Is he not coming?" Her voice rises an octave, and the nurse pulls the curtain open, the hospital gown on, and Madisyn's clothes in the middle of the floor.

"He's on his way."

"Well, tell him to hurry up!" Another contraction causes her to moan and double over in agony.

"You'd better get here before the baby does," I say.

"Yes, boss," Luka jokes with me before ending the call.

The nurse checks Madisyn's vitals. I give her a few minutes while I pick up her dirty clothes from the floor, place them inside a plastic bag, and then glance out into the hallway. No sign of Mikhail yet.

"Is he here?" Madisyn asks, glancing at me from the bed.

"He will be," I say, reassuring her that everything will be fine. Mikhail isn't going to miss the birth of his first child, no matter what.

I don't dare admit I'm jealous that Luka wasn't there when Bay was born. It's not the least bit his fault or mine. I tried to track him down, but he was a difficult man to find.

And now, I don't want to be anywhere else but with him. We've been taking things slow since Mark's death, which is best. Jumping head-first into a relationship may have felt good initially, but we both have Bay to think about. Plus, because we barely know anything about one another, it's hard for it not to be about lust.

And lust isn't long-lasting. With Luka, I want more. Forever.

"I'm here!" Mikhail rushes into the room and brushes past me, giving me a nod. "Thanks," he whispers and hurries to Madisyn's side, taking her hand.

I don't want to intrude. I quietly step into the hallway. I'm near the door if Madisyn needs anything, but she has Mikhail, the nurses, and the doctor.

I give her space, privacy, and time for them to bond. Pretty soon, it'll be three, and their lives will forever change.

———

"Did I miss the birth?" Bay asks as Luka carries her down the corridor. She's cuddling a stuffed teddy bear from the gift shop, the tag still on its ear.

I have a feeling they grabbed the gift for the new baby, but if I'm right, Bay isn't going to want to part with it.

"Trust me, you don't want to see it," I joke, smiling at Luka and Bay. "Thank you." I appreciate that he took the time to pick her up, doubling back since he was already going to the concierge center with Mikhail.

"Of course. How is she?" Luka asks.

"Madisyn or the baby girl?" I ask.

Luka smiles a genuine grin. "Wow. Mikhail must be surprised. He swore it would be a boy. I should have taken his bet."

"But you're a good man," I say, rising up on my tiptoes and kissing him. "And do you really want to piss off your boss?"

"Good point."

"Mama!" Bay holds out her arms, wanting to get down from Luka as she climbs onto me like a little monkey.

"How was preschool? Did you have fun?" I ask.

"Can I have a baby sister?" Bay asks.

"That's an excellent question," Luka says, a wry grin on his face.

"Did you put Bay up to this?"

Luka holds his hands up in surrender. "I plead the fifth."

EPILOGUE

Luka

Six Weeks Later...

"Are you sure you want my help?" Madisyn asks as we stare at diamond rings behind the jewelry counter. This is the fifth shop that we've wandered into this afternoon.

She glances at her phone, distracted.

"Hannah and Mikhail can handle Kira." It's not a surprise that she's worried. It's the first time she's left the baby and gone out on her own. Although, technically, she isn't alone. She's helping me shop for an engagement ring.

"I've just never left Kira alone."

"Do you think Mikhail can't handle the baby?" I ask.

"No, he's quite capable. I just miss her already."

"Good, then help me pick out an engagement ring, and we can head home."

She laughs. "This could take a lifetime at the rate we're going. Does Hannah know we're shopping for rings?"

I pause when I see the perfect ring and ask the jewelry store attendant to retrieve it from behind the glass.

"She doesn't even know that I'm planning to propose."

"Details!" Madisyn swoons. "I'm still waiting for Mikhail to propose, but it hasn't been that long. You two, you've been together only a few months. Don't you think it's too soon?"

She ogles the engagement ring as the jeweler retrieves it from the case.

"Quit trying to give me cold feet. I love Hannah and want to spend the rest of my life with her and Bay.

Besides, we're trying for another baby, and before that little one appears, I want to make it official."

Hannah may have been engaged once before, to Mark, but she'd intended to marry him for stability, not love. I don't have those reservations about our relationship. She's made it clear that she loves me both in and out of the bedroom.

I don't have Mark's problem, the inability to make her scream my name in ecstasy. No, it's quite the opposite. It's a struggle to keep her quiet when I bring her over the edge, so she doesn't wake the entire compound.

"How are you going to propose?" Madisyn asks.

I examine the ring. It will look amazing on Hannah's hand. It's white gold and gorgeous, with a large diamond in the center and smaller diamonds around the band. It costs more than I care to admit, but she is worth every cent.

"I haven't gotten that far," I say. "Do you think she'd prefer a grand gesture or something small and private?"

"Hannah seems more like a small and private proposal type of girl, but I want the grand gesture if Mikhail asks."

"I'll be sure to let him know." I laugh and roll my eyes. I thoroughly inspect the ring again, making sure it's flawless. "I'll take it."

———

Thank you for reading Wicked Boss. I hope you enjoyed Luka and Hannah's story. Want to read the proposal and see more of your favorite characters? Continue the adventure with Nikita and Lucy in *Possessive Boss*.

Lucy Quinn

I've made a few bad decisions in my life. At the top of the list, attempting to rob the Russian Bratva. I wasn't aware who I was robbing or what I was getting myself involved in until it was too late.

The guards with guns at the entrance should have been an indicator to walk away.

But now I can't leave.

I'm in deep with the bratva, forced to work for them, under Nikita Krylova.

Nikita Krylova

The little spitfire thought she could steal from me, blindly rob us, and not have to be punished.

Lucky for me, the pakhan, Mikhail Barinov, has let me choose how to handle our little five-foot-three, dark-haired, green-eyed problem.

She's feisty, insolent, and brazen.

I'm just the man to tame her.

Break her.

And make her mine.

Possessive Boss is the third book in the Bratva Brothers series. It can be read as a standalone and contains no cheating, no cliffhanger, and a happily ever after ending.

GIVEAWAYS, FREE BOOKS, AND MORE GOODIES

I hope you enjoyed Wicked Boss and loved Luka and Hannah's story.

Sign up for my Willow Fox newsletter

If you enjoyed Wicked Boss, please take a moment to leave a review. Reviews help other readers discover my books.

Not sure what to write? That's okay. It doesn't have to be long. You can share how you discovered my book; was it a recommendation by a friend or a book club? Let readers know who your favorite character is or what you'd like to see happen next.

Thank you for reading! I hope you'll consider joining my mailing list for free books, promotions, giveaways, and new release news.

ABOUT THE AUTHOR

Willow Fox has loved writing since she was in high school (many ages ago). Her small town romances are reflective of living in a small town in rural America.

Whether she's writing romance or sitting outside by the bonfire reading a good book, Willow loves the magic of the written word.

She dreams of being swept off her feet and hopes to do that to her readers!

Visit her website at:

https://authorwillowfox.com

ALSO BY WILLOW FOX

Eagle Tactical Series

Expose: Jaxson

Stealth: Mason

Conceal: Lincoln

Covert: Jayden

Truce: Declan

Mafia Marriages

Secret Vow

Captive Vow

Savage Vow

Unwilling Vow

Ruthless Vow

Bratva Brothers

Brutal Boss

Wicked Boss

Possessive Boss

Obsessive Boss

Dangerous Boss

Bossy Single Dad Series

Billionaire Grump

Looking for kinkier books? Try these spicy stories written under the name Allison West.

Boxsets

Academy of Littles

Western Daddies Collection

Obey Daddy Collection

The Alpha Collection

Western Daddies

Her Billionaire Daddy

Her Cowboy Daddy

Her Outlaw Daddy

Her Forbidden Daddy

Standalone Romances

The Victorian Shift

Jailed Little Jade

Prefer a sweeter romance with action and adventure?
Check out these titles under the name Ruth Silver.

Aberrant Series

Love Forbidden

Secrets Forbidden

Magic Forbidden

Escape Forbidden

Refuge Forbidden

Boxsets

Gem Apocalypse

Nightblood

Royal Reaper

Royal Deception

Standalones

Stolen Art

www.ingramcontent.com/pod-product-compliance
Lightning Source LLC
Chambersburg PA
CBHW021035030726
47496CB00006B/1553